The Royal Diaries

Kristina

The Girl King

BY CAROLYN MEYER

Scholastic Inc. New York

Sweden,
1638

June 21, 1638 — Midsummer Day
Castle of the Three Crowns, Stockholm

I never did go to bed at all last night. Who wants to sleep when the sun scarcely sets and the sky is bright?

The servants put up a great spruce tree in one of the castle courtyards and decorated it with hoops and ribbons and gilded eggs and Sweden's beautiful blue-and-yellow flag on top. My cousins and their friends danced around it until they could barely stand. I did not dance. As my mother often reminds me, I am as awkward as a newborn colt, and it is better that I just watch.

Margareta, my serving maid, says that in her village bonfires are lit at every crossroads on Midsummer Eve to cancel the power of the evil Trolls. I tell her no Trolls dare come to Stadsholmen, the island on which the king's castle stands, and we need no bonfires.

Now everyone has gone to bed exhausted. I shall stay awake and write in this lovely book of blank pages, a gift from Aunt Katarina in celebration of Midsummer Day.

"What shall I put in it?" I asked her, for I have never had such a book, each page white and perfect.

"Fill it with good and honest words, from your heart as well as your mind," said my dear aunt. Then she took my face in her hands and kissed me tenderly.

She might have added, <u>Do not show it to your mother.</u> But there was no need to say it. I have not seen my mother for nearly two years.

June 22, 1638

It is now just four hours past midnight, and the sun rides high above the horizon. I love this bright, silent time before anyone is up and about, except the castle guards and some very clamorous birds. I have resolved to set aside these early hours for writing in this book.

I have thought it over carefully. In a few years, I will be of age to rule, and since I mean to be a great ruler — certainly as great as Elizabeth of England (and she was merely a <u>queen</u>!) — I have decided to make a record of my life, beginning not just today but with events in the past that have led to the present. Students of history who read of Kristina of Sweden will know the true story, written by her own hand.

I will say this at the outset: She hates me. It is because I am a girl and ugly.

I speak of my mother, the Dowager Queen Maria Eleonora. She desperately wanted a boy, you see. A son.

Naturally, so did my father, Gustav II Adolf, King of Sweden. He needed an heir to succeed him and become the next king. In fact — is this not hilarious? — at first my father believed I <u>was</u> a boy! At my birth on the eighth of December 1626, I was covered from my neck to my knees with a caul, a membrane that hid from him the vital difference. And Frau Anna, my old nurse, often told me that as a newborn babe I had a very loud, deep voice.

For a brief, joyful time, my father believed that his prayers had been answered. He had a son! From the highest noble to the humblest peasant, all of Sweden rejoiced!

But others recognized the truth: I was undeniably FEMALE, and the king must be told, even as he was drinking to the health of the future king. Finally, my father's older sister, Katarina, carried me to my father and held me up, naked, so that he could see for himself.

He set down his goblet and stared. Then he said (and these are his exact words): "Let us thank God, my sister. This girl shall become as good as any boy. I ask God to preserve her, since He has given her to me." He named me Kristina, in honor of his own strong-willed mother, and ordered all the celebrations customary for the birth of a prince. Three weeks later, he summoned the Riksdag, the great assembly, the ruling body of five hundred men, to meet in Stockholm. There he declared me the future king of Sweden.

King. Not queen. Queens are merely the wives of kings and of no importance — I care not what anyone says.

My father may have been well pleased with me, but my mother was not. The astrologers had promised that I would be a boy, and she had dreamed every night of a son. After my birth eleven years and some months ago, my mother was inconsolable. According to Frau Anna, she wept without ceasing for three days and nights.

How grateful I am to be with my aunt and her family — and not with my mother!

June 25, 1638

To tell my story, I must go back to my great-grandfather, Gustav Eriksson, crowned king of Sweden in 1523. He used a *vasa* — a sheaf of grain — as his emblem, and at his coronation he took Vasa as his name as well.

King Gustav Vasa married three times and had three

sons who succeeded him — Erik, Johan, and Karl. After King Gustav's death, the crown passed from one son to the next. The youngest, King Karl IX, died in 1611, when his own son, my father, was just sixteen.

My father, the young new king, Gustav II Adolf, was a bold and gallant military leader. As he grew older, he won the hearts of his people as a fair and just ruler. Because of his courage and his flowing golden hair, people called him "The Lion of the North." After he was killed in battle nearly six years ago, he became known as Gustav Adolf the Great.

I am next in the Vasa line of rulers. Although I have officially held the title of king since my father's death, by law I cannot rule until my eighteenth birthday. More than six years to wait!

June 26, 1638

While I lived with my widowed mother, I often dreamed that I was falling. My own screams woke me and my old nurse, too. Her nightcap askew, Frau Anna would glare at me and grumble, "What is it now?"

One good thing about those terrible dreams: My mother no longer insisted that I sleep in her bed. Instead, she ordered me to sleep with Frau Anna.

I could not tell my mother that Frau Anna herself was the cause of the dreams, for she was the one who dropped me when I was just an infant. (She does not think I remember, but I do!) Frau Anna let me fall to the ground, and my shoulder was injured and could not be made right. To this day, that shoulder sags painfully.

Everyone claimed it was an accident, but I believe otherwise. Frau Anna had accompanied Maria Eleonora from Berlin when she married my father, and she saw my mother through two miscarriages and the death of a one-year-old daughter before I was conceived. Perhaps Frau Anna could not bear the idea that I was another disappointment to my mother and dropped me on purpose.

There were other incidents as well. Shortly after my christening, when I was only a few days old, a heavy beam fell across my cradle. The cradle was smashed to splinters, but I was unharmed. Evil spirits, I was told, but I do not believe that either.

June 27, 1638

This is the view from my open window: Sunlight glitters on the waters of the harbor where Lake Mälaren flows into the Baltic Sea. Deep blue surrounds Stadsholmen and the many other islands and rocky skerries of Stockholm. Three Crowns Castle is vast, with a great round inner tower, all protected by thick walls and a deep moat. Ships of every kind lie at anchor. I love to see the forest of masts, wind filling the great white sails as the ships leave the harbor, bound for faraway ports.

When I was not yet three years old, I stood at this same window and watched my father sail away to lead our armies in defense of our Protestant cause. I worshiped my father. During the deepest winter months when fighting was suspended and my father was at home, he spent several hours each day with me, telling me stories of our Viking ancestors and the ancient Norse gods, like Thor, the god of thunder, and Odin, the god of war. When he was gone, I missed him dreadfully.

My mother sailed with him on that warship. She put me in the care of my father's sister, Aunt Katarina, and my uncle, the Count Palatine Johann Kasimir, while she accompanied my father to Germany. (Any excuse to leave Sweden! She has always disliked living here and makes no apology for it.)

For months she stayed in a town far from the front lines, welcoming my father back after each victorious battle. I did not miss my mother, even at my tender age, for I was too busy basking in the warmth of my aunt's love and approval.

Then, on November 12, 1632, my father met his death. Surrounded by a heavy mist, he had become separated from his soldiers. Hours later, his horse galloped back to the Swedish lines with his pistols still in the holsters. When his body was found, he had been stabbed in the chest and shot in the temple and plundered of everything but his shirt.

More later. Papa Matthiae, my tutor, is here.

Midnight

On my sixth birthday, December 8, the news of my father's death reached Sweden. I heard it from Aunt Katarina. We clung to each other and wept. I wanted only to stay in the comforting circle of her arms, but suddenly everyone was kneeling before me, kissing my hand. Even Uncle Johann, a powerful nobleman, knelt and pledged me his loyalty. I had no time to mourn my father's death. I was now king!

Early in February 1633, I was presented to the Riksdag. I am told I showed a great majesty that struck awe into the hearts of nobles, clergy, burghers, and peasants, the Four Estates of the Riksdag. But there was one exception. A representative of the peasant class, Lars Larsson, rose slowly to his feet. "Who is this daughter of Gustav Adolf?" he asked gruffly. "We do not know her and we have never seen her."

In reply, I hopped down from the huge throne, and the marshal escorted me right up to the big, raw-boned peasant. "Well," said Lars Larsson, peering at me closely, "there are the chin, the forehead, and surely the nose of our beloved Gösta Hooknose." (This was the people's affectionate name for their beloved king.) "I say, let her be our Queen." The peasant bent his stiff old knees and knelt at my feet, and I was acclaimed.

I did not think it was necessary to correct him: <u>king.</u> The one who rules.

June 28, 1638

The heart beats loudly in the golden casket above my mother's bed. I scream and put my hands over my ears. "It is your father's noble heart!" my mother cries. She presses a pillow over my face to stop my screams.

Last night I awoke, tangled in my bedcovers and sick

with fright. "The horrible dream again!" I sobbed when Gunilla, my new nurse, swept open my bed curtains and peered in.

Gunilla understood at once what was happening. "Be gone, vile creature, in the name of God!" she cried, facing each corner of the chamber in turn and making the sign of the Cross. Then she lay down by my side and stroked my brow to soothe me until, at last, I slept peacefully.

Gunilla says my terrible dreams are caused by a spirit creature that comes in the night to haunt my sleep. She does her best to drive away these night-mares, as she calls them, and I am grateful to her. (Did cruel Frau Anna understand that? If she did, she never told me.) Gunilla claims that such creatures exist to make our hard lives even harder — as do the fiendish Trolls.

June 29, 1638

Still I am tormented by the most terrible memories of my father's death and of what happened afterward.

In the spring of 1633, six months after his death, we received word that my mother would accompany my father's body from Germany. My uncle and aunt traveled with me to the royal castle in Nyköping, to await the arrival of the warship that would bring my father's embalmed body and my grieving mother home.

For weeks we waited at the castle. I dreaded seeing my mother again, but my aunt reminded me that, as much as she loved me, it was my duty to be with my mother. Then, on this very day five years ago, the ship arrived. The sun was bright, as it is today, and my heavy mourning robes and veils were hot and painful on my crippled shoulder. I held fast to Aunt Katarina's hand until she gently pushed me forward. Sobbing loudly, my mother swept me into her embrace.

We escorted the coffin, placed in a black carriage drawn by six black horses, from the ship to the castle in a solemn procession. "From now on," said my grief-stricken mother, "you will live at Nyköping with me."

My mother ordered the walls and windows of the royal apartments to be draped in black velvet. All was darkness. My father's coffin, decorated with pearls and surrounded by candles, stood next to her bedchamber. Hour after hour, my mother wailed her great grief, sometimes pausing to crush me to her perfumed bosom and drench me with her tears.

"Your dear father's heart was placed in this golden vessel," my mother told me, her pale face swollen with weeping. "I shall always keep it with me by my bedside."

That is when the night-mares began to visit, and I dreamed that I could hear my father's heart beating like a drum in the golden vessel that hung above us.

June 30, 1638

My father's last wish was that my aunt and uncle be responsible for my care in the event of his death. But my mother refused to abide by his wishes, claiming that it was cruel to separate her from her only child. She banished Katarina and Johann and their children to their castle in Stegeborg, two days' journey south of Nyköping.

My heart was breaking when I bade my aunt farewell. As I clung to her, she whispered that she would write to me often. She kept her promise, secretly sending the letters in care of my tutor. Always she added the good wishes of my cousins — Karl, Marie Euphrosyne, Eleonore, and Adolf Johann — saying they all prayed for the day we might be together again. And, in fact, one day we were. But that did not happen for a long time. Only her letters saved me from complete despair.

My mother's deep mourning continued for twelve more months. I was a prisoner of her anguish. Night after night, for a whole year I was forced to lie in the great bed by my mother's side, listening to her sobs and praying that my aunt would find a way to rescue me. My mother's outbursts of grief frightened me.

For an entire year my mother refused to allow my father's body to be buried. During the night she would climb out of bed and, kneeling by the coffin, carry on long conversations with his departed spirit. At last, she would return to the bed we shared. When she touched me, her hands were cold as death.

Finally, she relented and allowed his funeral and burial to take place. The coffin was carried on a black-draped barge from Nyköping to Riddarholm Church, in Stockholm, accompanied by a cortege of funeral barges that stretched as far as I could see. Once inside the church, she demanded that the coffin be opened one more time so that she could say a last good-bye to my father's long-dead corpse. The bishop who preached that day was hard put to make himself heard above my mother's piteous wails. I still shudder at the memory.

My mother kept me with her for two more unhappy years. Most of the time she ignored me. Yet every day she summoned me and, in front of her court, chastised me for my untidiness. She pointed out that my hair was uncombed, my fingernails ragged, my petticoat rumpled. "You are worse than any boy," she complained. "A hoyden!"

No doubt I was! No doubt I still am.

Later

Yesterday my cousin Karl challenged me to a race, which I won easily. Now he wants to race again tomorrow, using different horses. I predict that the results will be the same. It upsets him when I best him at these challenges, because he is four years older and thinks he should be able to defeat me. He cannot.

July 2, 1638

I bested Karl again — hardly a surprise — but he is furious at being beaten by a <u>girl.</u> Now he proposes that we shoot at targets from our horses, and I have agreed.

Before my father sailed away that last time, he drew up plans for my education. I was to be trained as a <u>prince,</u> not a princess, and taught those things that a boy of noble birth must master. He assigned Axel Banér as my governor. Captain Banér is an excellent huntsman and soldier, but he is hot-tempered and vulgar, poorly educated, and unable to speak any language but Swedish. Still, he is the main reason I can outride Karl and — as Karl will soon find out — outshoot him as well.

My father also appointed a subgovernor, Gustav Horn, to teach me languages. He is a brilliant man of the world who speaks several tongues, although I have heard that he is overfond of drink.

Johannes Matthiae, who used to be my father's chaplain, is my principal tutor. (I call him Papa Matthiae because he has become nearly like a father to me.) He arrives early in the morning and stays with me until our midday meal. We are studying the Roman historians, the Psalms of David, and Aesop's Fables, all of which I enjoy very much.

And, most important, there is Axel Oxenstierna. He was my father's chancellor and is now chairman of the Committee of Regents, five men appointed to rule Sweden until I come of age at eighteen. Every afternoon the chancellor comes to instruct me in the art of governing and in matters of foreign and domestic affairs.

My mother <u>hates</u> Chancellor Oxenstierna, because he is the reason I once again live with my aunt and uncle and not with her. Later, I shall explain why. Just now I must go out to give poor Karl a lesson in marksmanship.

July 3, 1638

"Please, Kristina, do not gloat!" Karl begged yesterday as we put away our pistols. I think he was relieved when it started to rain so hard that we had to give up the contest, for I was already well ahead in points.

Two of my cousins will join me for lessons with Papa Matthiae: Marie Euphrosyne and her younger sister, Eleonore, who is just my age. Little Adolf Johann has his own tutor, and Karl studies at the university at Uppsala.

Marie Euphrosyne is sweet-tempered and lively, like her mother, my aunt. She is also intelligent but lazy and once complained to Papa Matthiae that she would surely become ill if she had to study such long hours as I do!

I said nothing at the time, but afterward I made my displeasure known to Papa Matthiae. He merely replied in his mild way, "Marie Euphrosyne will never rule her country. What does it matter whether or not she memorizes the speeches of Julius Caesar?"

Eleonore is a rather dull and placid girl who swears that she truly enjoys embroidery! How can anyone "truly enjoy" such a meaningless pastime? Her only dream is to marry a rich nobleman and bear many children. I have not told her that I think she is a fool.

Now my cousins have returned to their own apartments

(I am happy to be rid of them, and they are even happier to go), and soon it will be time for Axel Oxenstierna's daily visit.

I have had this book only a week, and already I have dropped a blot of ink on it!

July 4, 1638

Chancellor Oxenstierna has been back in Sweden since the summer before last, after several years of tending to our country's interests abroad. Before his return, my mother and I had moved here to Three Crowns from Nyköping. I had my own royal apartments, but my mother would not permit me to stay in them. She allowed me to come here only for my lessons, which were my only escape from her suffocating attention.

On the chancellor's first visit in 1636, my mother demanded that I receive him in her chambers. Then she proceeded to berate me for my appearance. My hair was unkempt, she said. My shoes were a disgrace — why had I not put on my new kidskin slippers? "Because these suit me better," I declared, kicking up my low-heeled boots.

But she had to stop her faultfinding when the chancellor was announced.

Oxenstierna thought I would not remember him after his long absence, but I did (I have an excellent memory). He is tall and straight as a fir tree, with stern gray eyes, great bushy eyebrows, and a beard streaked with white. His manner is grave and rather chilly.

The chancellor greeted my mother with respect, but it was <u>me</u> he knelt before, <u>my hand</u> he kissed. I stole a peek at my mother's face, which was pinched in an unpleasant scowl. But that scowl was nothing compared to the look she gave the chancellor when he dismissed her and her gaggle of German ladies-in-waiting, politely, but firmly. He wished to speak to me alone.

No time to write any more now.

July 6, 1638

This was what the chancellor said:

"Before your father left Sweden, he seemed to know that he would never see his beloved homeland or you, his cherished daughter, again." He explained that my father had given him charge over me, to prepare me to be the next ruler of Sweden, and that the Råd — the king's privy council — had drawn up plans for my education.

The men of the Riksdag were in agreement with my father that I am to be brought up as a <u>prince</u>. The only female qualities those gentlemen wish to be cultivated are virtue and modesty. But above all, said Oxenstierna, they are concerned that I remain devout in the Lutheran church, the only faith permitted in Sweden.

Then the chancellor glanced away. "It pains me to say this, Kristina," he murmured, "but the esteemed gentlemen do not wish you to be unduly influenced by the queen, your mother."

"They do not like her, do they?" I asked bluntly.

The chancellor sighed. "They fear that she is lacking in emotional balance," he explained. Then he added, "And they also question her loyalty to Sweden."

His words dismayed me. I thought of what I had often heard her say: <u>I would rather dine on water and bread anywhere else than on royal fare in Sweden.</u> I remarked that it was true that she disliked Sweden. But did such a judgment mean that she was disloyal?

"Perhaps," he said.

There is more to record of this conversation. I shall continue it tomorrow.

Later

My cousin, Marie Euphrosyne, is such a silly creature! She giggles constantly, and she is not serious about our studies. Today, for example, she refused to get out of her bed until hours after I had been at my books. Then she yawned for another hour or two and complained that she was cold and hungry, or in some other way indisposed.

July 7, 1638

More about Chancellor Oxenstierna:

For several minutes after he talked about my mother, neither of us spoke. Then he looked me over carefully, from my drooping hair ribbon to my muddy boots, and asked me if I enjoyed good health.

I assured him that I did now but had once been ill for weeks. I had refused to drink the ale served me at each meal, for I loath ale as well as wine and all strong drink. I wanted water, which I was forbidden, for it is unhealthful. Then I found the rosewater that my mother kept to beautify her complexion and I crept into her bedchamber to drink it.

"I was thirsty," I explained to the chancellor.

One of my mother's serving maids caught me, and

when my mother heard what I had done, she took a birch rod to me. I still wince at the memory of the rod stinging my legs. I made up my mind to drink no liquids of any kind, and that is when I fell ill.

The chancellor asked what I now drink. "Small beer," I said, "but only because I must."

He asked many other questions, especially about my mother, and I spoke to him honestly of my feelings. He listened attentively, thanked me for my replies, and told me that we will see much of each other, for it is his duty to teach me what I need to know to become queen.

"King," I corrected him. Had he already forgotten that my father and the Riksdag intended that I be brought up as a <u>prince</u>? "I shall become king, as my father wished."

At this he merely nodded, although I thought I detected a slight smile, and the conversation ended. I am still not finished with this tale, but it is time now for my Latin studies. I hope Marie Euphrosyne shows more sense today than she did at yesterday's lesson.

Midnight

She did not. I have already spoken to Papa Matthiae of Marie Euphrosyne's indolent habits. If she does not mend her ways, I shall send a note to her father and ask him to tell his daughter that she must improve her behavior.

July 9, 1638

The new fencing master, Signor Guillermo Tagliaferro, reached here last week from Italy, and my instruction began yesterday. At the first lesson, Signor Tagliaferro advised me that there is much to learn in the art of fencing, that fencing is much like chess, that it first began with the Egyptians but was brought to its highest form by the Italians, and so on. He talks too much, in my opinion. I have not yet been allowed to even <u>touch</u> a sword!

I planned to challenge Karl before he leaves again for the university, but if Signor T does nothing but lecture, Karl may be gone before I learn anything useful.

July 11, 1638

Karl's friend, Magnus De la Gardie, arrived two days ago from his family's home at Läckö Castle on Lake Vänern. I was happy to see him, for I am tired of having only girls for companions — not only my two female cousins, but the half dozen ladies-in-waiting who trail around after me, including the Oxenstierna girls, nieces of the chancellor. Their infatuation with needle and thread drives me to distraction. I am much happier being with boys.

After my lessons yesterday, I persuaded Magnus and Karl to go riding with me. It occurred to me that if I were disguised as a boy, I would be free to ride however I liked. When we met at the stables, I was dressed in boy's breeches and doublet, "borrowed" from my youngest cousin, Adolf Johann, who is about my size. Magnus was much entertained by my disguise and presented me with a hat with a large feather. He and Karl agreed that I did look like a boy, and a handsome one at that! I decided to call myself "Gustav," and they promised to say nothing that would reveal my true identity.

My costume completely fooled the stable boys. I did not ask for my usual mare, but said I would ride Mjölnir, a fiery stallion. The stable boys readied the horses, assuming that "Gustav" would want a man's saddle. I have always used a lady's sidesaddle and had never ridden astride, although I have long wished to try it. We leaped onto our mounts, and off we flew. I knew immediately that I would never again willingly use a sidesaddle. At last, I was free!

We rode for hours, until my two companions begged me to return to the castle. The stable boys greeted us with rough jokes and the coarse language that young men often use among themselves. I felt myself blushing deeply, but then I decided to return their banter in kind. Magnus and Karl turned to stare at me when they heard my words and then bent over in howls of laughter. I sauntered off with them, boldly shouting a few more oaths over my shoulder as I did.

I ran to the place where I had hidden my clothing and quickly changed into my kirtle. I encountered Margareta as I hurried into the castle. "Madam!" she shrieked. "Whatever have you done to yourself?" And she dragged me off to brush my hair without waiting for a reply.

July 12, 1638

My aunt keeps a sharp eye on me. I think she suspects I have engaged in some impropriety. Unfortunately, I happened to use within her hearing some of the coarse language that I learned from the stable boys. Aunt Katarina blinked, looked at me hard, and blinked again. I think I have convinced her that she <u>misheard</u>.

"You must watch your words, Kristina," my cousin Karl warned me later. I know he is right.

July 13, 1638

Karl came to call upon me yesterday afternoon. He complains about his tedious studies at the university and admits that he will be happy only when he is finished. He plans to leave on a foreign tour lasting at least two years. How I envy him!

Oxenstierna arrived during Karl's visit. He treats Karl with extreme politeness, but I recognize that his civility is a mask to conceal his dislike.

"You do not approve of my cousin," I said after Karl had taken his leave. "Why not?"

"I do not disapprove of Karl," said the chancellor, "but I am concerned that he is overfond of you, and that his family may have the idea he will one day marry you."

"Marry me!" I cried. "Why would he want to do that?"

"In order to become king."

The chancellor explained that many noblemen, both here and abroad, will be eager to marry me with the intention of ruling Sweden. I said nothing, for I know this will never happen. I will be the king, and no one will rule for me. The idea of a husband is completely ridiculous. I am sure Karl would laugh at it, too.

July 14, 1638

My mother has written me a letter, stained with tears shed because she is separated from her only child, her beloved daughter. She reminds me that we have been separated for nearly two years and implores me to visit her. I have sent a reply promising that I will, without saying exactly <u>when</u>.

I dread it.

July 17, 1638

Now I shall record how and why my mother left Stockholm.

By the autumn of 1636, nearly four years after my father's death, Chancellor Oxenstierna had been coming to my apartments nearly every day to instruct me. One day, the chancellor told me that I was to accompany him to the royal castle at Uppsala, two days' journey to the north.

As usual, I was attended by my tiresome retinue of ladies-in-waiting, serving maids, and all the rest, but I had learned to ignore them. This was my first visit to Uppsala, and I was happy simply to enjoy the passage through Lake Mälaren on the royal barge and then up the River Fyrisån to the old city.

The castle stands on a hill, overlooking the town. Most of the houses, built of logs caulked with moss, had turfed roofs upon which nimble-footed goats were grazing. Soon after we arrived, Oxenstierna took me to the splendid brick cathedral and showed me the King's Vault, near the main altar, where every king of Sweden has been crowned. When I closed my eyes, I could imagine myself seated beneath the soaring dome, the crown being placed upon my head, the scepter in my hand.

Later we visited the enormous Hall of State of the castle where kings are enthroned after their coronation. I shall be seated here, I thought, and I could almost hear the crowds roar: Long live King Kristina!

After two weeks in Uppsala, I asked the chancellor when we might return to Stockholm. His reply: We would stay where we were until the dowager queen — my mother — had packed her belongings and moved with her ladies-in-waiting and her servants from Three Crowns to Gripsholm Castle.

Gripsholm! This was a surprise to me. Why, I asked, had the dowager queen decided so suddenly to leave Stockholm? If she must live in "uncivilized Sweden," as she calls it, then my mother has always insisted on dwelling in the city, not at the western end of Lake Mälaren, which might as well be the end of the world.

"It was not her choice," the chancellor said. "It was mine. And not mine alone — the Råd has ordered it."

Then I understood the reason for our journey: to allow the Råd to send my mother away. To banish her!

At first I was troubled. But, as time passed, I realized I would at last be free of her smothering attentions that began when she became a widow, as well as of her endless criticism. She is my mother and for that I owe her respect. But I did not, and do not, want to live with her.

It will be two years in September since my mother left for Gripsholm. I have not seen her in all that time.

July 21, 1638

A very early visit from Axel Banér, who first taught me how to shoot both pistol and musket. Now he lectures me on the types of cannon best suited for various kinds of military action and how to position them in battle.

Sunset

Fencing progress: Signor T demonstrated several basic positions and moves — on-guard, advance, retreat, attack, parry, and thrust. I am to practice using <u>a broomstick</u> as a weapon. When will I be ready for a sword?

July 24, 1638

This is my name day. Everyone who bears the name of Kristina celebrates the feast day of this saint, born long ago in Italy. Cristina (as it is spelled in Italian) was the daughter of a rich man who kept a number of golden idols in his house. Cristina smashed the idols and gave the gold pieces to the poor. For that, she was tortured mercilessly. Her father, who ordered the torture, was so angry with her that he died of spite. Is that possible, I wonder — to die of spite?

Later, I told the story of Saint Cristina to Adolf Johann, who promptly burst into brokenhearted sobs. I felt sorry that I had done it and found my little cousin a sweetmeat to stop his wails.

July 25, 1638

A gift has arrived from my mother: A gown of green-and-gold brocade with a tight-fitting waist, gold-laced over a kirtle of red silk, the whole stitched with gold thread and little pearls and other jewels. The white lace collar is very fashionable and scratchy. I detest it.

With the gift came a letter begging me to arrange a visit to Gripsholm. This time my mother offers no harsh words of criticism, just a yearning to see her only child. I fear that I shall have to do this soon.

July 27, 1638

Karl and Magnus persuaded me to assume my "Gustavian" disguise and go to the stables with them. This is the only way I can ride astride without upsetting everyone. I rode the magnificent Mjölnir, and we had a splendid time.

Magnus is a handsome fellow, much wittier than Karl, and once again there was a great deal of hilarity and ribald language. I uttered some colorful oaths, mostly to watch the expression on Karl's usually sober face.

July 30, 1638

Someone reported my offensive language to Aunt Katarina. I suspect that Karl confided to Marie Euphrosyne (or maybe it was Magnus, keen to make a good impression on her). Marie Euphrosyne no doubt rushed to tattle to her mother. I have never seen Aunt Katarina so distressed. Usually, she is good-natured, but this time she decided I must be punished. I learn my punishment tomorrow.

July 31, 1638

She took a birch rod to me! How dare she! But I refused to shed a single tear, although Aunt Katarina herself was weeping. Worse, and more painful, I am forbidden to visit the stables.

I am so angry that I may just go to Gripsholm and stay there! My mother surely would not have me birched merely for speaking carelessly. When I next see the chancellor, I shall inform him that I wish to be taken to Gripsholm as soon as possible. I have already sent a letter to my mother, thanking her for the "beautiful" gown (it is truly a horror), and telling her that she may expect a visit from me soon.

August 2, 1638

I have decided to forgive Aunt Katarina. Oxenstierna has convinced me, without much difficulty, that I do not really want to live at Gripsholm. But now I have promised my mother a visit, and there is no way out of it.

August 3, 1638

Papa Matthiae arrived last evening, accompanied by Jakob Henrik Elbfas, the court painter. I feared this meant I should have to pose for another official portrait. They dress you in wretchedly uncomfortable gowns and make you stand perfectly still for hours, holding something in your hand — a large feather, or a glove, or some symbolic object. When you think you cannot bear it for another minute, the thing is finished, and you are expected to say how splendid it is!

As it turns out, Herr Elbfas is not here to paint my portrait, but to instruct me in the art of painting. I may take some pleasure in that, but in truth if I am not with Papa Matthiae and studying a serious subject, I prefer to be outside and on horseback, if possible. Or with a fencing sword.

August 7, 1638

I told Herr Elbfas that I wish to paint a portrait of my father. But he says I must first master basic techniques, and instead he had me paint a tree! I cannot see how painting a tree will help me learn to paint my father's likeness.

August 13, 1638

More fencing progress: I have been practicing the "on-guard" position, stepping forward and holding my "weapon" at the level of Signor T's chin. Today I learned the lunge.

"Free arm up and out of the way, behind your head!" shouts Signor T. This is to present your opponent with the smallest possible target. "Now LUNGE!" I have practiced the lunges and do exactly as he tells me. "Again!" he cries.

Still with a broomstick.

August 14, 1638

Poor Margareta! I lunged at her, nearly frightening her out of her wits, which are not especially sharp to begin with. Then I realized it was wrong of me to scare her, and I apologized sincerely.

August 15, 1638

Another letter from my mother, expressing gladness that I have promised to come soon. She writes (again!) how much she hates Gripsholm, she suffers from the dampness in summer and the cold in winter, there is no gaiety in her life, her heart is broken, and the fault must be laid at the feet of Axel Oxenstierna, who has separated her from her beloved child and sent her into exile. Et cetera, et cetera. Then, seeming to forget her joy at my coming visit, she delivers a lecture on the need to change my collars and cuffs more often.

Sunset

Still painting trees! Soon I shall have created an entire forest and nothing else.

Last night I found a rare moment alone with my aunt, as she sat stitching on a piece of needlework for the chapel altar. I asked her to tell me more about my mother and father.

Aunt Katarina laid aside the stitchery. "Gustav Adolf was only sixteen when our father died of apoplexy and he became king," she said thoughtfully. "I myself was twenty-six at the time, and not yet married to the count."

She told me the king soon fell in love with a beautiful girl named Ebba Brahe, a member of the court of Dowager Queen Kristina, his mother. The queen had taken over Ebba's upbringing after the death of Ebba's own mother. But Queen Kristina opposed the match, because Ebba was not of royal blood. She refused to give her son permission to marry Ebba.

For years the two lovers wrote secretly to each other, while Gustav Adolf patiently tried to persuade his mother to approve the marriage. Still she refused. She had been told by an astrologer when her son was born that he would not marry until he reached the age of twenty-five. All the queen had to do to get her way was put off granting her blessing for a few more years!

"Your father obeyed his mother's wishes," said my

aunt. "There were tears in his eyes when he told me he had sent his sweetheart a letter of farewell."

Soon after, Ebba was betrothed to one of Gustav Adolf's generals, Jakob De la Gardie. Ebba and Jakob were married on Midsummer Day 1618. Gustav Adolf did not attend the wedding. He had gone to sea on the trial voyage of a new warship.

"Ebba is the mother of Karl's friend, Magnus De la Gardie — she was your father's first love," said my aunt.

I wonder if Magnus knows this.

Sunset

I have advanced from painting trees to painting flowers in a vase. Dull, dull, dull! I might as well be embroidering.

August 17, 1638

Here is Aunt Katarina's story of my father's marriage:

Months passed after his twenty-fifth birthday, and my father had not found a bride, although he knew it was his duty to marry and provide a successor for the welfare of the country. But he could not marry just anyone. It had to be a good political match.

His advisors suggested a suitable young woman in Berlin, the sister of the Elector of Brandenburg (Electors being the most powerful princes in Europe). In the spring of 1620, Gustav Adolf traveled in disguise to Berlin, calling himself "Captain Gars." "Gars" stood for "Gustavus Adolfus Rex Sueciae," my aunt explained — Latin for "Gustav Adolf King of the Swedes." Captain Gars was introduced to Maria Eleonora and found her both beautiful and charming.

The princess fell instantly in love with the dashing young officer with the great mane of golden hair. The king revealed his true identity, and when he returned to Sweden that summer, he instructed his chancellor, Axel Oxenstierna, to negotiate a marriage contract.

A few months later, Maria Eleonora and her attendants stepped ashore at Kalmar, south of Stockholm on the coast of the Baltic Sea. Her future husband greeted her and took her to Kalmar Castle, the finest castle in all of Sweden. All kinds of wonderful banquets and celebrations had been arranged to entertain the bride.

The royal party traveled to Stockholm for the wedding on November 25. Gustav Adolf had the walls and ceilings of Three Crowns painted, new tapestries hung, the store-rooms stocked with fine imported wines. But the bride hated the castle. She hated the entire city built on islands.

<u>How could she hate it?</u> I wondered. <u>It is so beautiful!</u>

But Stockholm was not like Berlin, with its paved streets and stately brick mansions, Katarina explained. Maria Eleonora found Sweden wild and uncivilized. She thought the same of the Swedes themselves. Ignorant peasants, she called them.

Nevertheless, the wedding took place, and three days later she was crowned queen. According to my aunt, Queen Maria Eleonora may have despised the Swedes, but she was madly in love with her new husband, and as long as he was by her side, she was happy. The dowager queen was also pleased: The astrologer's prediction had been fulfilled. Gustav Adolf was married before his twenty-sixth birthday.

August 20, 1638

Before Karl left yesterday for Uppsala to resume his studies, he asked if I would take care of his hunting dogs. I promised I would, and gladly. I am banned from the stables, but Aunt Katarina has not said anything about the kennels.

Karl does not name his hounds, but instead he numbers them. My favorite is Seven, a harrier with silky, drooping ears and a sweet disposition. Seven would not be my favorite dog for hunting, for he is an indolent fellow, but he will lie perfectly still and let me paint his likeness. So — from trees to flowers to hounds. Herr Elbfas claims to be pleased with my progress but says I am not yet ready to begin a portrait of my father.

August 22, 1638

The chancellor does not like my plan to visit my mother, but he has agreed to arrange the journey. Papa Matthiae will accompany me, to be sure I do not fall behind in my studies and to keep a keen eye on my mother.

Before I leave for Gripsholm, I must appear before the Råd for the oral examinations to which I am subjected three times a year.

August 28, 1638

The sun rises about four hours past midnight. By this time tomorrow we shall be on our way to Gripsholm, and so there is much feverish preparation for the journey.

Adolf Johann is happy to watch over Karl's dogs in my absence, although it will fall to the master of the hounds to make sure all goes well. I did not ask either Eleonore or Marie Euphrosyne to do it. The poor animals would surely expire before either one of those silly girls took notice.

Aunt Katarina has gone over my wardrobe with extraordinary care, examining my shoes, mending my gowns, even buying me new ribbons for my hair. "To please your lady mother," she says.

I am more concerned about the oral examination this afternoon, although I am well prepared, of course.

Sunset

If those old graybeards thought they could frighten me, they were entirely wrong.

There they sat, all robed in black, lined up like sober judges about to examine me regarding some terrible crime. They receive daily reports from Papa Matthiae that explain precisely what studies I have undertaken and how well I have mastered them. But still they ask tedious questions! Johan Skytte, who was my father's tutor, always asks me about the teachings of Erasmus, the humanist scholar from Rotterdam. And, as usual, one of the burghers from the province of Dalarna, who is more interested in war than in theology, asks me about the campaigns of Alexander the Great.

I could see that I had impressed them well and proved that I am as fine a scholar as any boy.

September 1, 1638
Gripsholm Castle, Mariefred

Here I am, once again under my mother's watch.

After warm good-byes from my aunt, we left Stockholm before a brisk wind, and the royal barge made good time under sail across Lake Mälaren. (The barge is carved and painted in bright red and yellow and decorated with the Vasa coat of arms.) At dusk, we headed for shore and were welcomed by Karl Karlsson, a nobleman whose mansion sits on a low bluff.

On the second day, the winds died and a light rain began to fall. The sails were lowered and the oarsmen took over. As the day wore on, the storm strengthened, whipping the lake into a boiling stew. The oarsmen managed to keep the barge on course, even though all aboard were more or less drenched. At last, we stepped ashore at the pleasant country mansion of Count Lars Sparre, a member of the Riksdag. This was the first time I had met his beautiful daughter, Ebba.

Generally, I dislike the society of women of any age and especially beautiful ones who make me even more aware of my own faults. But Ebba has a sharp wit, and I truly enjoyed her company.

The rain slackened by the morning of the third day, and we moved like a ghost through a heavy veil of mist and fog. At last, the sun broke through to reveal the magnificent old castle, its majestic round towers and cupolas reflected in the shimmering water of the lake.

I took a deep breath and prepared for my mother's tearful greeting. But that is not what happened.

More later.

September 3, 1638

I expected my mother to greet me when I arrived, but instead, she sent word that I was to call upon her when I was ready. And when I was ready, she was not!

At last, she was waiting to receive me in her chambers, dressed in silk and velvet and laden with jewels, as though she presides over the finest court in the world. (My father never liked to wear jewels or ornaments — not even a ring on his finger or a golden chain over his coat.) But my mother's is not a fine court — it is a very strange one. Her courtiers are dwarfs and hunchbacks, more than I would have thought existed in all of Sweden, every one of them arrayed in a costume of motley and jingling with jesters' bells.

Since my earliest childhood I have feared these various buffoons, whose role is to entertain the queen and her ladies. My mother knows of my fears. When I was still a little child, she instructed Frau Anna to carry me to each one of them for a kiss. I began to howl long before I had finished the ordeal.

"Will you not kiss them, Kristina?" my mother called out now from the shadows.

I could feel myself beginning to tremble. I do not know if these are the same creatures I was forced to kiss as a child, but their faces were stretched in those same grimaces that make a mockery of laughter.

"I kiss only you, Your Majesty," I replied and hurried past the dwarfs and hunchbacks to kneel at her feet. With a cry she seized me, and her sobbing began.

So, nothing has changed. Had I really believed it would?

September 6, 1638

Thank goodness Papa Matthiae is here with me, and I do not have to spend every waking hour with my mother.

Not that she seems happy to see me, after all. First drowning me with her sentimental tears, she then began clucking and scowling at my appearance.

"You look like a common peasant!" she cried. "And a dirty one at that!"

I was dressed for traveling in a petticoat of woven wool and a shawl of the type worn by Margareta, my serving maid. I find these more comfortable than the lavish gowns favored by the ladies of the court. My mother called for a comb and began tugging it through my unruly hair. She sent for one of her serving maids and had her scrub my hands with perfumed soap, slather them with some foul-smelling grease, and put gloves on me so that I would not soil whatever I touched.

Then the lectures began, on how I must try to become more <u>feminine</u>.

No matter how much my mother urges me to take up such feminine pursuits as embroidery, she herself has no patience for it. Everywhere there are piles of her needle-work, unfinished and forgotten. The one thing that seems to hold her interest are sweetmeats, into which her delicate white hand is continually dipping. I am forbidden to have any — impossible while wearing gloves!

September 10, 1638

Besides Papa Matthiae, my only other escape from my mother is a daily walk with Gunilla and Margareta in the castle gardens.

Gripsholm is as handsome a castle as I have seen, the walls and wooden ceilings beautifully painted, the floors intricately inlaid with patterns of wood. It was built three centuries ago by a nobleman as a place of refuge and later donated to a monastery. Later still, it was a royal prison — my father's uncle was imprisoned here by another uncle. Then it became the "queen's dower," to be given to the king's widow upon his death. That is how it came to my mother, who insists that it is still a prison and she is a prisoner.

September 13, 1638

Screeches, cackles, hoots, jeers. The grotesque creatures caper around me, catching at my sleeves, pulling my hair, grabbing my hand, trying to drag me into their mad dance. My mother laughs, her mouth open wide, as she urges them on. I try to flee, but my feet are too heavy to move.

"Your untidy hair!" cries my mother.

"Hair! Hair!" shout the creatures.

Another terrible night-mare, and I wake up sobbing. Gunilla tries to drive it away, claiming that it comes because of the full moon. I know otherwise.

I have been here at Gripsholm for nearly two weeks, so miserable that I can hardly bring myself to write in this book. I flee to Papa Matthiae for help, though there is little he can do but offer understanding.

September 15, 1638

A large and splendid portrait of my father hangs in the Great Hall, where we take our meals. I remember when he posed for that portrait. I had watched him don thick padding under his coat in order to achieve the fashionable rounded shape, and Herr Elbfas gave me a stool to perch on while he painted. My father seemed to enjoy having me there with him.

"She will undoubtedly be a clever woman, for even at her birth she succeeded in deceiving us all," he told Herr Elbfas. Then my father looked at me with great love. "She is already a clever child." Always, when I study this portrait, I feel his clear, calm gaze upon me.

This gave me an idea. I have brought pigments, oils, brushes, and boards supplied by Herr Elbfas, thinking I might fill my time with more trees and flowers and even a dog, if I could find one. But my original desire was to paint a portrait of my father, and I think now that I might use the portrait hanging in the Great Hall as my model.

I plan to work in secret, early in the morning, before my mother is up and about. Tomorrow I begin.

September 18, 1638

It is not only the way I <u>dress</u> that displeases my mother, but also the way I <u>walk</u>. "What an awkward child you are," my mother sighed yesterday. "Show me your shoes."

Reluctantly, I raised my skirt to my ankles and allowed her to see my shoes, low-heeled and square-toed. I like them because I can move about in them quickly.

"A man's shoes!" she shrieked. "Take them off this instant!" There was another shriek when she observed that my stockings were coarse wool and none too clean.

My mother sent me to put on stockings made of embroidered silk and a pair of her own dainty satin slippers with pointed toes and delicately curved wooden heels. For a full hour she had me walk back and forth in front of her. The shoes pinched painfully, and I found it hard to balance on the narrow heels.

"Glide, Kristina, glide!" she entreated me, getting up to demonstrate. Now every day I am to have what she calls "lessons in feminine grace."

September 19, 1638

The lessons have begun.

"You are hopeless, Kristina!" my mother cries, as I attempt to glide in a manner that will please her. I fail, again and again. She is right: I <u>am</u> hopeless.

I miss my aunt desperately. I would even be happy to see my cousins.

But the secret portrait of my father is progressing. I rise at my usual time of four hours past midnight and wake Margareta. The two of us creep to the Great Hall. We light candles to illuminate the portrait on the wall, and then Margareta keeps watch for my mother or one of her servants. Small chance that any of them would be up at such an hour, but we take no risks.

Midnight

I accidentally tore a hole in the silk stockings. It is not a big hole — just big enough to change my mother's mind about continuing my lessons in feminine grace.

September 21, 1638

My mother announced yesterday that the time has come to begin thinking of the choice of a husband. <u>My</u> husband.

I made no response. I thought it would be a relief to have our conversation shift from my shortcomings, but this was not the subject I wanted.

"I am certain," she said, "that the Kasimirs would like nothing better than to have you marry their son, Karl. And I can think of nothing worse."

Still I said nothing, for I know that Oxenstierna shares her opinion of my aunt and uncle Kasimir. Is it not ironic that the chancellor and the dowager queen, who despise each other, think alike on this matter?

Ignoring my silence, my mother pressed on. "Young Karl Gustav is a pleasant fellow," she continued. "I have always thought so. But it must be said, Kristina, that he is not the brightest candle on the table."

I felt that out of loyalty I should leap to Karl's defense. He is highly intelligent. It is only that his manner of speech is slow and deliberate. In our childish games I was always the leader, mainly because I talk so much faster. However, Karl's intelligence, or lack of it, is not the point. I am not in the least interested in marrying Karl, or anyone else. Besides, when he finishes his studies this spring, he plans to leave for a tour of the Continent to gain military experience.

"I am too young to think of marriage," I said quietly but — I hoped — firmly.

"Then others must think of it for you," my mother replied. I must be sensible, she says, and she reminds me that it is my duty to marry and to provide a successor to the throne. I know that. I remember well Aunt Katarina's story of my grandmother's influence on my father's marriage. The evidence is here before my eyes.

Then, smiling slyly, my mother told me that she has someone in mind who would be entirely suitable: her nephew, Prince Friedrich Wilhelm of Brandenburg.

Suddenly, I burst into tears. I could not help it. In disgust, my mother sent me away.

September 22, 1638

Papa Matthiae was not pleased when I told him about the conversation with my mother. He assures me that no decision will be made for some time. I have nothing to fear, he says, for a suitable husband will surely be found for me.

This was still not the answer I wanted.

"But I desire no husband at all!" I cried, stamping my

foot. At that, Papa Matthiae merely raised his bushy eyebrows and clicked his tongue — <u>tsk, tsk, tsk!</u>

September 26, 1638

The portrait progresses slowly. Maybe Herr Elbfas was right — I have not mastered the basic skills, for my father's noble features are still unrecognizable in my painting.

October 1, 1638

I have been at Gripsholm for a month, and I cannot bear it even one more day! I have begged Papa Matthiae to take me back to Stockholm. He promises that we will leave by mid-month, but even that is not soon enough.

It rains nearly every morning. Although I plead that I cannot be kept cooped up like a caged bird, my mother forbids me to walk outside when it is raining. This gives her another chance to complain about Sweden's gloomy weather. In Berlin, she says, the months of autumn are beautiful, with clear, bright days and cool nights. According to my mother, everything in Germany is better than it could ever be in Sweden.

My mother insists that we dine formally every day, the table in the Great Hall covered in a damask cloth that is put into the linen press after the meal to restore the perfect creases. The table is laid with damask napkins folded in fanciful shapes that she reminds me are <u>not</u> to be used. We are served great platters of eel pies, meat stews, and fermented herring, but my mother is interested mostly in the sweets. My stomach churns.

October 12, 1638

We've postponed our departure because Gunilla has fallen ill.

My mother hovers over Gunilla, wringing her hands, even though she makes no secret of her dislike of my nurse. If I did not manage to drive my mother from the bedside, poor Gunilla would get no rest at all.

My mother reminds everyone, loudly, that in Germany and other parts of what she calls "the civilized world," there are skilled barber-surgeons who cure patients by bleeding and other scientific means and apothecaries who concoct miraculous potions. But here in "this wretched country" we must depend upon the mercy of God and the help of a few ignorant countrywomen with their herbs and poultices and superstitious incantations.

October 29, 1638

I have not written in this book for days, because most of the time I have no wish to spoil the perfect white pages with my own black thoughts.

Gunilla is much improved, and Papa Matthiae has informed my mother that we plan to leave tomorrow. The results were predictable. The weeping and lamenting began immediately. My mother's suffocating love for me nearly drives me to despair. Sometimes it scares me.

Sunset

She found the painting.

I made the mistake of not putting it back in its hiding place in the larder quickly enough. Now she talks of nothing else, flattering me that it is an excellent likeness of my father, claiming that she loves it so much she cannot bear to let me take it away.

I have pointed out that she has several portraits of my father while I have none, but the rivers of tears continue to flow.

November 3, 1638
Sparre Manor, Horn

What a dreadful scene! My mother became hysterical when the time came for me to board the royal barge. I tried to calm her with promises to come back in the spring. She says she will keep the unfinished portrait of my father for me to finish when I return. The painting is a hostage that she holds to force me to come back.

We traveled for only one day before the weather turned against us. Papa Matthiae ordered the boatmen to put in at Horn, so that we might again accept the hospitality of Count Sparre and his family. We have been here since.

Ebba comes to visit me as soon as I finish my lessons with Papa Matthiae, and we talk while the wind howls outside and sleet rattles against the windowpanes. Ebba was born the same year I was, but in January, and so is well past her twelfth birthday while I still wait for mine. Although she is neither vain nor silly, she is truly beautiful. Every feature from brow to chin is so well formed that Herr Elbfas would no doubt give the world to paint her.

November 7, 1638

Papa Matthiae points out that winter is upon us, and we must leave at the first break in the weather, before the lake freezes. Maybe as soon as tomorrow.

November 10, 1638
Castle of the Three Crowns, Stockholm

I shed no tears when I left my mother at Gripsholm, but I shed many when I said farewell to Ebba. What a splendid friend! She will come to Stockholm with her father in January when the Riksdag convenes, and she has promised to write to me in the meantime.

The weather held, we broke through the crackling skin of ice that formed overnight on the lake, and the wind was at our backs until we were safely home. I was happy to see the dear faces of my aunt Katarina and my uncle Johann. I even found myself welcoming the silly prattle of my cousins, and wanting to hear news of Karl and Magnus, who will be here at Yuletide.

I am so happy to be home again. My beloved aunt greeted me as she always does, taking my face in her two hands, as though it were something very precious and not at all displeasing!

November 12, 1638

A sad day: the sixth anniversary of my father's death, to be observed with special religious services.

My aunt remarks that I look pale and thin, and she has concluded that large draughts of mead will restore me to health. I have told her I will take no fermented drink, but Gunilla is also insistent on the healing properties of the honey brew. Next, I expect them to force me to drink the milk of a cow! Margareta claims that in the countryside many people drink this, and goat's milk as well, and prosper from it. What a revolting idea.

Aunt Katarina herself might benefit from such a

drink. She looks very tired, although she denies that anything is wrong.

Sunset

I managed to pour out the first cup of mead, but Aunt Katarina suspected as much and has ordered Margareta to stand by to make sure I swallow it. Cow's milk could not possibly taste any worse.

The service in memory of my father was morbid and gloomy. Why can we not celebrate the joy of his life instead of the grief of his death?

November 13, 1638

When Chancellor Oxenstierna inquired about my mother, I told him that she spoke of arranging a marriage for me with her nephew, my cousin Friedrich Wilhelm.

"Do not concern yourself, Kristina," the chancellor said in what I suppose were meant to be comforting tones. "We intend to find you a proper husband, and your mother will have nothing to say about it."

"But I do not want a husband!" I nearly shouted at

him. I regret my outburst, but not the cause of it. It is becoming clear to me that everyone, without exception, is determined that I must have a husband, whether I want one or not, for the sake of the realm.

Midnight

Snow has been falling all day, and I took Karl's hounds out for a run in it. When I returned to my chambers, I was wet to the skin. This greatly alarmed Gunilla, who warned me at great length of the dire consequences of being wet, until I had to beg her to be silent.

November 17, 1638

Eager to resume my fencing lessons, Signor T armed me with my broomstick and we practiced "disengagement," flicking the "blade" from left to right and back again. All well and good, but when will I get to use an actual rapier with a real blade?

Axel Banér appeared on Saturday morning for my riding lesson. (I am allowed to go to the stables now, if properly accompanied.) When I was six years old, Banér taught me how to sit well in a sidesaddle. He was aghast when I confessed that I had been riding Mjölnir with a man's saddle and preferred it.

"But Madam, you cannot!" he stammered.

I reminded him that I am being raised as a <u>prince</u>, not a princess, and therefore I should ride astride like any boy. "It is what my father would want!"

Poor Banér! He coughed and stumbled in his speech and stared at his boots and finally managed to say that riding astride would certainly impede my ability to bear children.

I laughed and said, "But I have no desire to bear children, sir!"

All the redness drained from his face, and he grew pale as ashes. "It is your duty to bear children, Madam," he croaked, "for the sake of the kingdom."

I realized at once that I should never have said any of it, since he is likely to report my words to the Regents. But it <u>is</u> the way I feel, duty or no.

November 20, 1638

I am back to my old habits of study. I had fallen into sloth during my stay at Gripsholm, when I was constantly at my mother's beck and call.

All is dark and still when I rise at four o'clock, dress in whatever comes to hand, and wrap myself in a woolen cloak. Then I throw open the window, regardless of the cold. When it is clear, the moonlight glitters on the harbor ice. On most days, I write a few lines or a page in this book before I plunge into my studies. The striking of the clock in the church steeple keeps count of the passing hours. The sun rises much later now, at nearly half past seven. By then, I have already been at my books for several hours.

When Papa Matthiae arrives, we begin my lessons. I have finished reading all ten volumes of Curtius's *History of Alexander the Great* and begun Livy's *History of Rome*, all in Latin, and I am memorizing parts of Cicero's *Philippics*.

Eventually, Eleonore dawdles in, and later Marie Euphrosyne makes her loud entrance. Work proceeds at a much slower pace with the new arrivals. Early in the afternoon Papa Matthiae departs and my cousins and I dine with my aunt and uncle, usually a simple meal of herring and potatoes.

Then Oxenstierna arrives. Papa Matthiae's method

of instruction — memorization — is an easy matter for me, but the chancellor approaches my education in another way. He describes the problems that a ruler may encounter — whether or not to go to war, for instance — and has me consider both sides of the question, weigh everything in the balance, and then arrive at a conclusion. At times, I am overwhelmed by the responsibility I shall one day carry, although the chancellor reminds me that I am my father's daughter in every way and will make a brilliant ruler.

November 21, 1638

My remarks to Captain Banér have reached the chancellor's ears. "The duty of every woman is to bear children," Oxenstierna intoned solemnly. "The duty of every monarch is to provide an heir to the throne. Do you understand that, Kristina?"

I said that I understood. "But cannot one provide an heir without actually giving birth?" I asked.

The chancellor reared back in his chair. "What are you thinking, Madam?"

It was simply an innocent question, but my words clearly upset the chancellor. He reminded me that the throne of Sweden has been hereditary since Gustav Vasa was king and that other branches of the Vasa family have sometimes laid claim.

"Your father was quite concerned that the succession be secured. That was why he had you declared his successor. And that is why it is your duty to marry and provide Sweden with its next king."

"But I do not want to marry, and I do not want to bear a child," I said in the calmest voice I could muster.

"You will change your mind," the chancellor said, forcing a thin smile.

I will not, I thought, and no one can force me. But I said nothing more. There must be another solution.

November 23, 1638

Chancellor Oxenstierna has arranged for a dancing master to come from France to introduce a kind of dance called *ballet*. "It will show the world that the Swedish court is as cultured as any in Europe," he announced grandly.

Try convincing my mother of that!

November 24, 1638

Today is Saturday, and I have spent the morning riding and shooting with the oafish Axel Banér. But this afternoon I shall be with my language tutor, Gustav Horn, who is the opposite of Banér: cultured, well-educated, and fluent in several languages. With him, I have studied Latin (I can write it as well as I write Swedish) and German (my mother's language — she refuses to read, write, or speak Swedish). Now I am learning French, the most beautiful tongue in the world.

Master Horn says I have a gift for languages, as did my father, who was proficient in seven and had some knowledge of several others. I have begun to study ancient Greek, and soon I want to begin Spanish and Italian.

"And English?" asked Horn. "Surely you intend to study the language of that great island kingdom? There was a talented dramatist of your father's and grandfather's generation, William Shakespeare, whose work you should certainly read."

"They have no culture to speak of," I informed him. "Although I do admire their former queen, Elizabeth."

What I did <u>not</u> tell him is that I admire Elizabeth mostly because she never married. If she could rule her country without a husband, then surely I can do so as well.

Later

For the first time, Signor T allowed me to handle the rapier! He said I did exceptionally well (this was no surprise), but he claims that is because of my long practice with the broomstick.

November 26, 1638

Yesterday, the Sunday before the beginning of Advent, we all marched off to church to hear the same tiresome sermon about the Last Judgment that I have been hearing for years.

When I was quite young, I had to listen to the terrifying story of the final trial of all people, both living and dead, at the end of the world. The preacher used such horrific images to describe it that I was certain heaven and earth would collapse that very night and bury me in the ruins. I wept, and Aunt Katarina had to console me.

The sermons are as terrible as ever, spoken in thunderous tones to scare us the more, but I am no longer frightened by these tales.

November 28, 1638

The dancing master, Monsieur Antoine de Beaulieu, has bulging eyes and a croaking voice and reminds me of a frog. He says that women do not take part in ballet. The roles of female characters are danced by men wearing wigs. So I need not pursue learning to dance.

Monsieur Antoine proposes to teach Karl and Magnus the new dance when they come from Uppsala.

December 1, 1638

Tomorrow is the first Sunday of Advent. Eleonore and Adolf Johann complain that they are forbidden cakes and sweetmeats until Christmas. "It is only four weeks," I remind them. "That is forever!" they moan.

December 5, 1638

The chancellor has decided it is time I study the other great kingdoms of the world, and he proposes to begin with an examination of Great Britain and the English monarchs. His particular favorite is Elizabeth.

I am interested in learning how the English queen managed to avoid marriage without making everyone angry.

December 7, 1638

Now I know! Elizabeth of England never actually <u>refused</u> to marry. Her advisors pressured her, and she let them believe that at anytime she might accept the proposal of the right suitor, for she had many (including my father's uncle, King Erik XIV). But the days and years simply passed by, and one day her advisors realized their queen was too old to bear a child and provide the realm with an heir to the throne. She proved to her subjects that she could rule as well as any man, and when she was on her deathbed she named her cousin as her successor. <u>There</u> is something to think about.

Tomorrow is my birthday.

December 8, 1638

TWELVE — at last! With each birthday I am closer to the day when I will actually reign as king of Sweden.

When my father was twelve, he received foreign ambassadors. When his own father lay dying, he addressed the Riksdag.

Papa Matthiae has said that in honor of the occasion, my lessons today will be abbreviated. Members of the Råd are expected to bring me greetings. And I hope for wonderful surprises — maybe a letter from my friend Ebba Sparre?

December 10, 1638

This is how I passed my birthday:

The entire De la Gardie family arrived from Läckö Castle. All fourteen children came, bringing with them an assortment of nurses and governesses for the younger ones and tutors and servants for the older ones. Three Crowns, which normally bustles and hums with the workings of government, but otherwise seems dull and cheerless, is suddenly a lively place.

Then I received a formal visit from the Regents and several members of the Råd, gentlemen in long black coats and tall-crowned hats, informing me that my presence will be welcome to open the next session of the Riksdag in January.

The banquet arranged by Aunt Katarina concluded with a sweets table (the Advent fast was lifted for one day). In the center was a cake made of sugar and almond paste, covered in a thin sheet of gold. The cake was surrounded by silver dishes of candied violets and figures molded of sugar dough and painted so cleverly that they seemed almost real. My cousins were ecstatic, and the children of the De la Gardie family could hardly be dragged away from it.

As for gifts: The chancellor gave me a woven tapestry picturing Alexander the Great, my most admired hero and ruler, next to my father. Papa Matthiae brought me a copy of the Lutheran catechism he has been preparing for years, copied onto vellum and bound in fine morocco leather. Marie Euphrosyne and Eleonore presented me with dainty handkerchiefs embroidered by their own hands, and my aunt had ordered me a pair of satin slippers (heaven knows when I shall ever wear them) as well as soft leather gloves lined with silk. My uncle Johann's gift is a handsome fur-lined cloak. From my mother came a miniature portrait of herself, mounted in a gilt frame set with many little jewels.

But my favorite gifts are from Karl, who presented me with a splendid silver rapier, etched with interesting designs, and from Magnus, who gave me a tooled leather scabbard for the rapier. (I immediately challenged Karl to a duel, and he accepted. We will meet after Christmas.)

Throughout the festivities I kept staring at Countess De la Gardie, the woman my father once loved and wished to marry. She is still a charming and lovely woman, with rosy cheeks and merry blue eyes. At last, I tumbled wearily into my bed and, as I lay there waiting for sleep, this thought came to me (and may God forgive me): <u>I wish my father had married her instead. I wish the countess were my mother.</u>

December 11, 1638

No message from Ebba Sparre. I am so disappointed. Could she have forgotten that it was my birthday?

December 12, 1638

A fierce storm swept in two nights ago, and snow fell steadily until late yesterday. The snow is too deep for the horses, who break through the icy crust and stand nearly up to their withers. Magnus proposed that we go out on skis, such as peasants use to get about in the countryside.

I was enthusiastic about this idea, and even Marie Euphrosyne and Eleonore agreed to try it. Soon, Magnus had us equipped with wooden boards strapped to our feet with leather thongs, and each of us had a branch stripped of leaves for pushing.

We were all clumsy at first, several times ending up facedown in the snow, except for Magnus. Eleonore soon complained of the cold and returned to the castle, accompanied by the Oxenstierna girls. To my surprise, Marie Euphrosyne stayed with us.

Once we mastered the art of it, we were able to cover a great distance in a short time. I remember my father's story of his grandfather Gustav Vasa, who narrowly escaped a Danish massacre in Stockholm before he became king. He was known as Gustav Eriksson when he tried to raise an army of Swedish peasants to fight against the Danes. At first, the peasants refused, and Gustav fled on skis toward safety in Norway. But the peasants reconsidered and dispatched two men on skis to catch up with Gustav and bring him back as their leader. The Danes were defeated, and two years later Gustav Eriksson became King Gustav Vasa.

I gained new respect for my great-grandfather and for the peasants who went after him when I discovered how hard it is to manage the clumsy wooden boards tied to my feet!

December 13, 1638

I understand now why Marie Euphrosyne attempted the skiing. It is because of Magnus. She blushes every time he looks her way, and I have noticed that he looks her way very often.

After dark

A letter from Ebba! A very short one, bringing her belated birthday greetings and promising that she will come to Stockholm with her father next month for the convening of the Riksdag. I am so pleased!

December 14, 1638

Last evening, as we warmed ourselves by the fire, Magnus described Läckö Castle. It has 240 chambers, or perhaps it is 280 (he is not sure), and many modern conveniences, such as freshwater carried by pipes from the lake to the kitchen and waste water carried out by the same means.

"But most of all, Marie, you would enjoy the swans that make their home there," said Magnus, smiling at Marie Euphrosyne as though she were the only one present.

"Does that include the dungeons?" I asked.

Everyone looked at me, startled by my question.

"I do not know," replied Magnus. "But all castles have dungeons. Surely there are dungeons at Three Crowns as well?"

"Yes, but I have never seen them."

Later, when I found myself alone for a moment with Karl and Magnus, I whispered, "Can we not visit the dungeons? The three of us, secretly?"

Karl and Magnus looked at each other and shook their heads. Karl began to object — mostly that this would be too upsetting for what he chooses to call my "delicate feminine sensibility." The more he protested, the more I insisted that I <u>would</u> go. I knew that I could convince Karl, just as I have always been able to persuade him to do what I want. Magnus is more stubborn.

"Why would you want to see the prisoners who are kept there? Nothing but thieves and petty criminals, the dregs of society!"

"Those prisoners are my subjects. I need to see the conditions under which they must endure their punishment," I said, to remind him that I am not just some foolish girl he can easily dismiss. I am his <u>king</u>.

"All right," sighed Karl. "Then we shall find a way."

December 17, 1638

Yesterday, after Sabbath services, Karl drew me aside. He and Magnus have devised a plan. We will visit the dungeons on Saturday, the night of the Winter Solstice. The tower guards will have been given their Yuletide allotment of drink and are likely to be drowsy. With the help of a ring of iron keys that Karl will somehow borrow from a guardsman, we will make our way to the dungeons. They promise to send me a disguise.

December 19, 1638

I have begun to regret my insistence on this adventure. Yesterday, Margareta brought me a bundle sent by Karl. I could see the question in her eyes when I laid it aside as though it were of no importance. As soon as she had gone, I opened the bundle: a guardsman's uniform. My disguise.

December 20, 1638

Eleonore is full of talk about the *tomten*, little sprites that she claims come each year at Yuletide. She has had her head filled with superstitious nonsense by one of her nurses. Eleonore insists that on Christmas morning we must leave the tomten an offering: a length of woolen cloth, a leather bag of tobacco, and a shovelful of earth.

I understand the cloth — to make himself a suit — and the tobacco (a plant brought from the New World — many of our men have taken to smoking the leaves in pipes, and the odor is loathsome), but why the shovelful of earth? Eleonore does not know. She claims to know what a tomte looks like, though: He is the size of a one-year-old child with a wizened face like a dried apple, and he wears a little red cap decorated with bells. Marie Euphrosyne and Adolf Johann are completely convinced, but Karl and I simply laughed at her.

"What is the name of your tomte?" I asked Eleonore, who turned quite pink in the face and burst into tears. Then I regretted teasing her.

Two more days until the dungeons.

December 21, 1638

I have finished writing the traditional Yuletide letters to members of my family. This year I wrote them in Latin, which annoys my cousins — especially Marie Euphrosyne, who complains that I try to make her and the others look bad. I denied it. It is not that I try to make her look bad — I try (successfully) to make myself look better. But I did not confess that.

"Tomorrow," Karl whispered as we left the hall where we had dined.

"I am ready," I said, more bravely than I felt.

December 22, 1638 — Winter Solstice

The fire in the hearth is nearly dead, only a few embers still glow, and my chamber is so cold that I can see my breath in the light of the candle.

This is the shortest day, with only a few hours of daylight. Around noon, the coppery sun creeps above the horizon, washing the walls of the castle in its pale glow. By three o'clock, it sinks and darkness comes again. This is payment for all the endless hours of summer daylight. I am told that in the northernmost parts of Sweden the sun barely appears at all in winter.

Tonight is the night in the dungeons.

December 23, 1638

Thank goodness, that adventure is over!

Last night, when I was certain that Gunilla was sleeping soundly, I slipped from my bed and dressed in my new disguise. The uniform proved much too large. Nevertheless, I belted the breeches tight around my waist and rolled up the legs. Then, with the cap slouched low over my brow, I crept down to the courtyard where Magnus and Karl were waiting.

Snow-filled clouds hid the quarter moon, and the night was very dark. When my two companions made out who I was, they laughed until they wept, which angered me. I refused to speak as we set off, although I could hear their snorts of suppressed laughter.

As expected, the guards were either sleepy or drunk or both, and we easily slipped by them and into the innermost courtyard where the Round Tower stands. Karl had bribed a guardsman for his keys, but he was not sure which key fit the heavy iron lock. At last, the right one was found, the lock yielded, the massive door groaned on its rusty hinges, and we stumbled inside.

All was blackness. I could see nothing, but I could hear the groans coming up through a grate in the floor. We were assaulted by foul odors so strong that I held my sleeve across my nose and mouth to keep from vomiting.

Karl lit a reed soaked in pitch and lowered it through the grate on a loop of wire. I could scarcely believe what I saw by that flickering light. Men in filthy rags squatted in the dark hole beneath the grate, gazing up at us with haunted, sunken eyes. They were not free to move about, even in the confines of that dreadful place, for all were shackled to the wall — some by ankles or wrists, one miserable creature chained by the neck.

"There are your subjects, Kristina," Karl whispered.

I heard other sounds, then: a quick scurrying. The light of the burning reed reflected in pairs of eyes as tiny as beads. Rats! Rats, everywhere!

I drew back from the horrible scene, and we left without another word. I hurried to my chamber where Gunilla snored peacefully, stuffed my disguise under my mattress, and climbed into my comfortable bed. Sleep would not come, as I lay wondering what could be done to improve the lot of those poor wretches, no matter how dreadful their crimes.

Midnight

I cannot remove thoughts of those miserable souls from my mind. Yesterday I spoke to Papa Matthiae of my concern for the poor unfortunates who suffer so, particularly at this time of year. I did not tell him, of course, how I know about their sufferings, but I did ask what could be done.

Papa Matthiae reminded me that he is my almoner, and as such it has always been his duty to distribute alms in my name. "At Yuletide, it is customary to give gifts of food and money to widows and orphans and others in need," he said.

"Prisoners, too," I begged. "Perhaps an extra ration of bread and some meat for those in the dungeons." Papa Matthiae looked at me curiously but asked no questions and promised to carry out my wishes.

December 24, 1638

Yuletide preparations have put everyone in a good mood. For the past few days, the cooks have been soaking slabs of dried codfish in a lye bath before boiling them, and I can smell the odor wherever I go. Tonight this *lutfisk* will be served with mustard sauce as the last fast of Advent.

For tomorrow's Christmas feast, we shall have, as always, roast suckling pig (I will not eat any; I detest pork). There will also be roast swan, as well as eel pies and oysters brought from the west coast of Sweden. I do not really care what is served — I would gladly eat oat porridge at every meal. I think of the poor souls in the dungeon, who may get only a bit of rotted meat and a scrap of moldy bread for their supper, despite my wishes.

Papa Matthiae says we shall have no lessons today or tomorrow. I hope to find someone willing to go out on skis.

Later

Karl and Magnus were willing, and we had a grand time — not so many falls headfirst into the snow this time. None of us wants to talk about what we saw in the dungeon.

December 26, 1638

Too much of everything — too many sermons that last too long, followed by too much eating and drinking. Margareta says that the snowy white feathers covering the roast swan are saved from one feast to the next. (I never knew that.) When the feathers are fastened in place, it is as though the cooked swan were still alive and swimming majestically on Lake Mälaren.

Uncle Johann played this prank: A pair of live pigeons had been given wine to make them tipsy, put into a pie dish, and covered with a crust. The pie was put into the oven and baked quickly so that the crust was browned but the birds were unharmed. Then the "pigeon pie" was presented, with a trumpet fanfare. My uncle made a great show of cutting open the pie and feigned amazement as the pigeons fluttered out and ran drunkenly across the table! Aunt Katarina plainly disapproves of such crude jests, frowning and refusing to join in the laughter. Claiming a headache, she left the hall. But the gentlemen at the table enjoyed it, cheering loudly and drinking a good many toasts to the health and good luck of the poor pigeons.

December 27, 1638

Yesterday was the feast day of St. Stefan, patron saint of horses. This gave my male cousins an excuse to run off to the stables. The female cousins naturally preferred to stay close to the stove with their needles and thread and gossip.

Magnus asked if I were going with them down to the stables. He was grinning mischievously, no doubt remembering the trouble I had gotten into in the past.

I went to ask my aunt's permission and to make the necessary promises to behave (and to speak) properly. But her servant told me she was resting and was not to be disturbed, so I decided to go without her leave.

The stable boys treated me with the deference due their monarch, no crude words escaped my lips, I rode sidesaddle, and it was scarcely any fun at all.

But tomorrow Karl and I meet for our fencing duel.

December 28, 1638

Ho! Bested him! Karl was astonished at how well I can parry and thrust, advance and retreat. I have more strength than Karl and can keep going long after he has tired and wants to quit. I think he regrets giving me that handsome rapier for my birthday. What made it worse for Karl (and more of a triumph for me) was that Magnus witnessed it all.

January 2, 1639

The New Year has begun. Gifts were exchanged last evening, a long and tedious event. I gave everyone silver spoons with the royal coat of arms (three crowns and the Vasa sheaf) and received the usual assortment of items. Every book, handkerchief, and glove had to be lavishly admired. I thought it would never end. I noticed that Aunt Katarina looked especially weary and slipped away early, as I wish I could have done. When I called at her chambers later, I was told that she had already retired.

January 4, 1639

Yesterday was my oral examination by the Råd. As usual, I left them all deeply impressed by the extent of my knowledge.

The chancellor reminded me that the Riksdag convenes on the fifteenth of this month, and I am expected to be present at the opening ceremony. As though I need reminding!

Soon I will see my friend Ebba. Her thirteenth birthday is tomorrow, and I have sent her a silver pomander ball in which to carry herbs to ward off harmful diseases.

January 7, 1639

Yesterday was the Feast of the Epiphany, a holy day observed by solemn sermons and long prayers, followed by Twelfth Night, an evening of raucous drinking and carousing, in which I took no part. (My aunt was present for only a short time. Who could blame her for not staying? But I thought she looked unwell.)

Worst among the drinkers, as usual, was Captain Banér, my governor in marksmanship and horsemanship. He is loudmouthed and vulgar. If he did not also hold the high office of Comptroller of the Royal Household, overseeing expenditures for every cup and coverlet and sack of grain, I would be happy to see the last of him.

January 9, 1639

Karl, Magnus, Magnus's younger brother Jakob, and even Adolf Johann have been spending hours with Monsieur de Beaulieu, practicing the ballet to be performed once the nobility has assembled in Stockholm for the opening of the Riksdag. They are even too busy to go skiing or riding!

January 11, 1639

Ebba and her family have arrived and settled into their handsome brick mansion not far from Three Crowns. I have invited them to attend the ballet tonight.

For days, Marie Euphrosyne and Eleonore have talked about nothing but the gowns and jewels they intend to display themselves in. Gunilla insists that I wear one of my elaborate gowns with lots of jewels and my new satin slippers. Margareta will do up my hair in curls and ribbons. I will endure it all in silence.

January 12, 1639

It turned out to be a splendid affair, all in my honor, but I would have enjoyed it more if I had not been laced into that dreadful gown so tightly I could hardly breathe. And those painful slippers! I wish my mother had been present to see that I looked quite presentable. But if she <u>had</u> been here, she would surely have found all kinds of things to complain about.

Many of our noble families, dressed in their most luxurious silks and furs and jewels, assembled in the Hall of State. Torches blazed in wall sconces. Ebba arrived wearing a gown of blue velvet. I sent her a note, asking her to come and sit with me, which she did. The court musicians started to play, the dancers made their entrance onto a stage built for the occasion, and the ballet began.

The extravagant costumes of the dancers created quite a stir. Karl and Magnus and the other young gentlemen were outfitted as huntsmen, and they moved around the stage in the most charming and complicated manner. Monsieur de Beaulieu had been drilling them for weeks in preparation for this evening, and the ballet master himself performed the solo dances and dazzled us with his brilliant leaps and turns.

I was thrilled by it all, and I was pleased that Ebba was there to enjoy it with me.

January 15, 1639

The Riksdag convenes in a few hours. I am ready to make my appearance and call for the official opening of the session. A part of me wishes that I could meet them today as their crowned ruler, and not just as a young girl in uncomfortable robes with no authority. That all belongs to Chancellor Oxenstierna and the Regents. But even as I wish for the absolute power once held by my father and grandfather and great-grandfather, the responsibility of wielding it truly frightens me.

And what does the chancellor still worry about most? The choice of my future husband! Apparently, the Regents agree that this is a serious subject demanding their attention <u>now</u>.

"If my father had not believed that I would be fit to rule as king, he would not have made me his heir," I told the chancellor.

"But he did not intend for you to rule alone, Kristina," Oxenstierna replied. I know he is probably right.

January 17, 1639

I do love to sit on the throne, the carpet of cloth of gold spread out before me with ninety liveried footmen lined up on either side, and that great crowd of men, some five hundred of them representing each of the four Estates, kneeling before me!

But then, when the ceremonies were finished and the men turned to the business of governing, I was invited to leave. Oxenstierna promises that in a year or two I will be called to attend the meetings of the Råd to observe their deliberations and, perhaps, to make comments of my own.

January 18, 1639

Karl and Magnus have gone back to the university, and the Countess De la Gardie and the rest of her brood are returning to Läckö tomorrow. By next year, the countess says their new palace, "Nonesuch," will be far enough along for them to stay there. The count has been building this palace in Stockholm for more than a half dozen years and it is still nowhere near completion.

Karl has promised to come down in a few weeks for the royal banquet on the night before the beginning of Lent. He wants to have another duel. He does not give up.

January 23, 1639

Sad news: Gustav Horn just brought me word of the sudden death of Axel Banér.

I feel very guilty, because I never liked Captain Banér, even though he was a fine and loyal soldier who always performed his duties well.

January 28, 1639

Axel Banér was laid to rest on Sunday, as is customary. All day Saturday I thought of him, and how well he instructed me in the so-called masculine arts. It is no doubt because of his patient training that I learned to ride and to shoot expertly. He was so proud that I could bring down a bounding hare with a single shot.

People from every class of society attended his funeral, and Gustav Horn spoke of him so eloquently that I felt a tightening in my throat.

January 31, 1639

Ebba called upon me yesterday, after Papa Matthiae had finished our lessons. I suggested a walk before the chancellor was due to arrive, but we had made only one turn around the courtyard when she began to shiver and begged me to return to my apartments.

There we found a message from Oxenstierna that he had business with the Riksdag and would not arrive until later. So that no time would be wasted, he had sent Herr Elbfas for a painting lesson, and I invited Ebba to join me.

She agreed, but her interest soon flagged. Instead, she offered to play the lute.

I found her an instrument, and Ebba began to play and to sing in a pure, sweet voice. I began a painting of the windmills I could see in the distance from my window, and so we passed a happy afternoon. Then the sun set, Oxenstierna returned, and that brief time of pleasure came to an end.

February 4, 1639

On Saturday morning I went down to the stables, where I usually met Captain Banér, but I felt so sad and lonely that I soon returned to my chamber. The arrival of Master Horn in the afternoon cheered me a little, and we spoke in French for the remainder of the day.

Last evening I went to visit Aunt Katarina. She seemed happy to see me, but it plainly cost her an effort to talk with me. She is pale with dark circles under her eyes and a languor that worries me. I asked if she were ill, but she shook her head. "Only a little weary," she said, forcing a smile.

February 10, 1639

For days I have brooded about my aunt, and finally I drew Uncle Johann aside and asked <u>him</u> if she were ill. He nodded sadly.

"But what is it?" I asked.

He explained that the physicians are unsure, suspecting something in the blood, and they are administering purgatives and leeches in hope of bringing some improvement. "We must pray, Kristina," he said.

February 12, 1639

Ebba was in church on Sunday with her parents. I noticed that she carried the silver pomander I sent for her birthday, and that she held it to her nose from time to time during the long (<u>long</u>!) sermon, to keep herself awake. I was glad to see her putting it to use.

It would take more than sweet-smelling herbs to soothe me. I cannot bear these sermons, so full of darkness and despair at a time when my heart is heavy with worry about my aunt. I have heard that the Roman Catholic church is a much more cheerful place than our dour and gloomy Lutheran houses of worship, but naturally I cannot say that to anyone. The Catholic faith is not permitted here in Sweden.

February 15, 1639

Each day my dear aunt seems to lose strength. I pray earnestly for her recovery. But suppose she does not improve? <u>Suppose she dies?</u> I cannot bear to think about what will become of me if my aunt leaves us. My greatest fear is that my mother would be given charge over me, and I would have nothing to say about it.

February 18, 1639

Karl sends word that he will be home from the university on Saturday, in time for the royal banquet before the start of Lent.

I thought there would not be a banquet, with Aunt Katarina in such poor health, but Chancellor Oxenstierna assured me that his wife, Beate, has taken over the planning. I do not much like her. Madame Beate is the dominant lady in the royal court, more highly placed than my aunt, and she owes her rank to being the wife of the chancellor. There is another reason for her position: Beate's husband is a Swedish nobleman, and Uncle Johann is a German citizen, invited by my father to live in Sweden after he and my aunt were married. I know that the chancellor is suspicious of Uncle Johann, not only because he is German but because he is suspected of not being steadfastly Lutheran.

It troubles me to be surrounded by such suspicions, but I am helpless to do anything about it.

February 20, 1639

Beate Oxenstierna bustles around Three Crowns as though it were <u>her</u> castle! She is tall and straight like her husband, with glittering gray eyes and a cold demeanor. She gives orders like a general in the field.

February 25, 1639

Karl arrived and was dismayed to find his mother in such weakened health. He is angry at Uncle Johann, at his sisters, and at me for not writing to tell him just how ill she is. He is also furious that Beate Oxenstierna is in charge of the banquet. He stamps back and forth, fuming, lower lip pouting, arms flailing, and, all in all, looking preposterous.

Then it was Aunt Katarina's turn to express annoyance. She told him to be quiet and to behave himself.

Magnus is here, too. It seems that Magnus misses no opportunity to visit, and I notice that Marie Euphrosyne is always <u>fluttery</u> when he is here. The De la Gardie family arrived en masse last week, and once again Three Crowns is bursting with life.

February 27, 1639 — Ash Wednesday

Thanks to Beate Oxenstierna, who outshone everyone with her magnificent jewels, last night's banquet was quite a lively and elegant affair. Ebba came to help me dress for the occasion, and that put Margareta out of temper. I told Ebba that I never devote more than a quarter of an hour to dressing, no matter what the occasion. She simply laughed.

"There is no point to it," I said, "because I am homely, and there is no help for it."

"You are not homely," said Ebba sternly. "You must never think that."

But, of course, I do. I have been told all my life that I am ill-favored. The proof is in the mirror.

"You have beautiful eyes," said Ebba. I argued that they are too large for my face, and that they are dark, almost black. My father had blue eyes. Most Swedes have blue eyes. Ebba herself has blue eyes. Why, then, are mine so dark?

Ebba shrugged and said they give me an air of <u>mystery</u>. And when I pointed out that my nose is much too big, she shrugged again and said that it has <u>nobility</u>. What about my complexion, which my mother complains is dark as a gypsy's? She thought for a moment and decided that it is <u>vivid</u>. My stature, I reminded her, is short and ungraceful. She replied that my hands are my best feature, very lovely and expressive.

Ebba begged me to allow her to arrange my hair, and so I sat patiently and let her do whatever she wanted with it. Once she had finished, she brought me a mirror. When I looked into it, I thought, at least for that moment, that I could see what she sees — if not a truly beautiful girl, then one who is surely not displeasing.

Later

Lent begins today: forty days of fasting and prayer, forty days of gloom. But I am still remembering the banquet.

While Ebba was deciding which jewels I should wear in my hair, trying first pearls and then emeralds, she asked if I were in love with Karl. The question took me by surprise, and I stood up so suddenly that the comb flew from her hands. "Of course not!" I nearly shouted. "Why do you ask such a question?"

She told me it is plain from Karl's face and manner that he loves me, but that my feelings are not so clear.

"Well, they should be," I said sharply. "I love Karl as one loves a brother. I have no intention of marrying him or anyone else. Ever!"

This seemed to amuse her. "You are only twelve. You are sure to feel otherwise when you are older."

I frowned at Ebba and explained that I want none of those things that seem to be expected of me. What I really want, I told her, is to be free of all restraints, so that I can do as I please, as long as I hurt no one. I have heard people say that kings have the power to do whatever they wish, but in fact the opposite is true: My life is governed by customs and traditions that I have no authority to change. There are so many things I cannot do, just because I am a woman!

I began to list for her all the things I could think of. Ride my horse astride. Use bad language, if I feel like it. Dress in men's breeches when I go walking. Travel abroad. I deeply envy Karl the journey he plans to undertake once his studies are finished in the spring. I would so love to visit France and Spain. And Italy! Especially Italy! I thought of Signor T, who has often told me of the magnificent works of art for which his country is famous.

"How wonderful if you would travel with me, Ebba!" I burst out suddenly.

Ebba smiled. "I have no desire for such a life," she said.

How is that possible? I wondered. I would have pursued this question had Gunilla not rushed in to remind us that the banquet could not start without me.

February 28, 1639

This is the last I shall write about the banquet:

The blare of trumpets announced the presentation of the festal peacock, roasted and stuffed and all its feathers replaced, including its colorful fan of a tail. Papa Matthiae gave the blessing over the food, and everyone ate and drank to great excess, as usual. It went on for nearly five hours, which is four hours too long for any occasion.

My aunt Katarina put in an appearance, leaning heavily on the arm of Uncle Johann, with Karl also supporting her. She smiled graciously, kissed Beate Oxenstierna on her dry cheek, and left soon after the presentation of the peacock.

Ebba sat with her parents and smiled whenever she happened to look my way. She could not sit with me because of royal protocol — who enters ahead of whom, who sits where and with whom, and so on, all so tedious.

The chancellor's wife, I am told, was appalled that I wore my usual low-heeled shoes. Margareta overheard her say to the wife of a nobleman that I should be ashamed to appear in such a state. I regretted only that I had not remembered to wear the satin slippers Aunt Katarina gave me for my birthday, because I know it would have pleased her.

March 4, 1639

Aunt Katarina has stopped coming to the table to dine with her family, claiming that it overtaxes her strength. I go to visit her every day, after my lessons with Papa Matthiae and before the chancellor arrives. She always says she is glad to see me, seems content to have me sit silently by her side for as long as I like, but never begs me to stay longer.

Yesterday, though, she said in her gentle voice, "Kristina, I want to tell you what your father was like when he was a boy."

"Yes, dear Aunt," I whispered, leaning closer.

She smiled. "He was never afraid of anything," she replied, "and he always knew he would be a great leader." She squeezed my hand. "You are like him." Aunt Katarina fell back against her pillow, exhausted, her eyes closed.

I kissed her and quietly left her chamber. Some days, I am confident that I will be a great leader like my father, and other days I am filled with doubt.

Oh, Aunt Katarina, do not leave me! I need you!

March 13, 1639

Two weeks of Lent are past, four remain. Aunt Katarina's condition has suddenly worsened. She no longer leaves her bed. It took courage for me to speak about my fears to Papa Matthiae. "Is she going to die?" I asked him.

"Only God knows the answer," he replied.

To me, that is no answer at all.

March 15, 1639

Papa Matthiae believes that the best course of action for me and my cousins is to apply ourselves fervently to our studies. I am to memorize the speeches of Caesar and Cato's debate in the Roman Senate. Poor Marie Euphrosyne! She struggles so merely to understand the Latin, and memorizing the speeches is completely beyond her powers even in the best of times. Eleonore drifts about like a ghost, her thoughts far away.

Then we move on to mathematics (algebra and geometry), geography, and astronomy. But, according to Papa Matthiae, examining the planets that streak across the heavens is of less importance than studying the Augsburg Confession — the beliefs and doctrines of our Lutheran religion — or the Bible. (I prefer the Old Testament. The Gospels are of little interest to me, but I keep that opinion to myself.)

No change in my aunt's condition, though my knees are nearly worn out with praying.

March 20, 1639

My mother has launched a new campaign of letter writing. Almost every day a messenger delivers another one. She wants to see me, she writes in one paragraph, because she loves me and she is being cruelly punished by people who despise her and will not let her be a natural mother.

Then, in the very next paragraph, she repeats her earlier complaints — that I am clumsy, awkward, careless, untidy, slipshod, shabby, ill-favored, ungrateful, bad-humored, and some others I have probably forgotten. And did I not promise months ago that I would visit her in the spring?

I scarcely know how to answer her. I showed one letter to Oxenstierna on his most recent visit. Suddenly, for no clear reason, I found myself weeping in front of the chancellor. "What is the matter?" he asked, looking uncomfortable at this display of passion.

And I, unable to hide my fears any longer, confessed that I have no idea what will become of me if my aunt dies, and I dread the thought that I might once again be forced to live under the same roof as my mother.

"No," he said firmly, "that will not happen."

But he did not say what <u>would</u>.

Yesterday was the Feast of the Annunciation, the day on which the Angel Gabriel visited the Virgin Mary to tell her that she had been chosen to be the mother of Christ.

Despite a chill wind, I persuaded Ebba to go walking. We had set a good pace, leaving the Oxenstierna nieces and the rest of my ladies trailing far behind. As we walked, I wondered aloud how the Virgin must have felt when she heard the angel's news.

"I think she was probably deeply pleased and honored. Would you not be?" Ebba replied.

"I cannot imagine why any woman would ever consent to go through the terrible business of bearing children," I said, lengthening my stride. "I will not have a husband, and I will not bear a child, and that is the end of it. It has to do with my temperament, which is hot and dry and, according to the physicians, does not favor childbearing."

As it happens, I am like my mother, who also has a hot, dry temperament. My mother lost three children before I was conceived, and I am sure that, like her, I would have great difficulty bringing a healthy child into this world.

The tip of Ebba's nose was ruddy from the cold. She nodded solemnly. "I see," she said, although I am not sure she does. I have no doubt that her temperament is cool and moist, like most women, and she will have no trouble bearing many healthy children. Maybe even fourteen of them, as the Countess De la Gardie has done.

Then I asked her if she knows about the custom among some Swedish people to run barefoot through the snow and slush on Annunciation Day, in order to toughen their feet. "Will you join me?" I teased. I knelt in the snow and began to unfasten my boots.

Ebba's blue eyes widened in dismay. "If you demand it, Your Majesty," she said bravely.

I laughed and assured her I would not ask her to do such a thing, even if I had made up my mind to do it myself.

April 6, 1639

Tomorrow is Palm Sunday, the start of the week of fasting and prayer in preparation for Easter. A few weeks ago, Gunilla gathered armfuls of silver birch branches to force the leaves. Now the branches are green, and we shall carry them in procession to the church in the morning.

Each time I visit Aunt Katarina, there seems to be less of her. It is as though the flesh were melting from her bones. Marie Euphrosyne says that her mother suffers greatly but never complains.

April 11, 1639 — Maundy Thursday

Last night as I returned from the chapel, I discovered Margareta searching for a place to hide her broom "So the witches cannot find it." She and the other servants are in a fright, for tonight the witches are said to gather in church towers and then fly to Blåkulla to practice their black magic and consort with the Devil.

I tried to talk reasonably to Margareta, asking exactly where is this "blue mountain." She claims Blåkulla is on an island somewhere near Kalmar.

"Nonsense," I said, but I did hasten to ask Papa Matthiae what he knows about Blåkulla.

"I know that the Devil exists," he said, "and there may be other evil beings as well." Then he changed the course of our conversation to the Crucifixion of Christ and the Resurrection, and I could get no more from him on the subject of witches.

April 13, 1639 — Easter Eve

When Karl learned that the servants' tales have alarmed his sisters and brother, he announced his plan to spend tonight in the tower of Riddarholm Church to prove that no witches gather there.

Marie Euphrosyne and Eleonore are in tears, but Adolf Johann is swollen with admiration for his courageous brother.

"In a short time I leave to visit the battlefields of the Continent," Karl says. "Surely I can spend a night alone in a church tower to prove that you are all being foolish."

April 15, 1639

"You are right! Witches everywhere!" Karl reported yesterday when the family, except for Aunt Katarina, gathered for our Easter feast. According to Karl, not only did the hags flock in great numbers to the church tower on Riddarholm, but he witnessed them scraping metal from the church bells and mixing the scrapings with other secret ingredients to smear on their brooms before they flew away.

Adolf Johann's eyes were round with wonder. "Did they speak to you?" the boy wanted to know.

"No," Karl replied solemnly. "I fired my pistol into the air, and the noise frightened them off."

Then Karl glanced at me and winked.

April 17, 1639

I am going to write this down, even if I can still hardly believe it happened.

Before Karl left for Uppsala, he begged permission to speak with me privately. I thought he wanted to confess he had invented the story of the witches in Riddarholm bell tower. Then I noticed his lower lip trembling, as it sometimes does when he is uneasy. So, I thought, his deception is really troubling his conscience!

"Dear Cousin," he began, shifting from one foot to the other. "It would please me greatly if you would —"

He hesitated and stared at his feet, as though the next words were written on the toes of his boots. Hoping to make the conversation easier, I said, "If I would forgive you for inventing tales of witches?"

He gaped at me, rubbed his nose (another nervous habit), and went on as though I had not spoken. "— if you would write to me during my absence. Because I cherish the hope that you might someday be kind enough to grant me a special place in your affections."

If I were a delicate sort, which I am not, I think I might have fainted dead away. What, exactly, did he mean, <u>to grant him a special place in my affections</u>? Is this his roundabout way of asking me to marry him? Surely not!

Recovering myself, I slapped him heartily on the shoulder and loudly promised to write to him, assuring him that I would keep him informed of events here in Stockholm. Then I hurried away as fast as I could.

April 19, 1639

My conversation with Karl has left me troubled. I care for him very much, more than I do Eleonore and Marie Euphrosyne. The reason is simple: With few exceptions men are far more interesting than women. BUT! An intellectual meeting of the minds with a man is one thing, and <u>marriage</u> is something else entirely. I hope that is not what Karl wants of me!

If only I could speak to my aunt about this, but she is far too weak for such a conversation.

April 20, 1639

Spring is on its way. Each day the sun rises earlier and stays up longer, and the fields are slowly turning green. Margareta has been anxiously waiting for the first cuckoo call of the year. She claims that if the call comes from the west, it is a sign of good tidings, from the east it means comfort and consolation, and from either north or south, it portends sorrow and death.

Last evening Margareta rushed into my chamber as I sat by my window, translating one of Caesar's speeches. I frowned at the interruption and was about to send her away, but she put her finger to her lips and shook her head.

I listened and heard the cuckoo's dull notes, coming from the north. My heart is heavy as a stone. I know what it means: Aunt Katarina.

April 23, 1639

I worry and pray, but Aunt Katarina seems neither better nor worse. If Uncle Johann or my cousins have heard the call of the cuckoo or noticed its direction, they give no sign.

April 30, 1639

The first of May is the Feast of Saint Valborg, and tonight — Valborg's Night — is another occasion for witches to make mischief. Karl writes from Uppsala that the students at the university observe this witches' sabbath by dressing in white and marching in procession from Uppsala Castle down to the river to celebrate, often quite raucously.

No raucous celebrations here. My aunt seems a little worse, and tomorrow I must appear before the Råd for my spring oral examinations.

May 2, 1639

Papa Matthiae had informed the members of the Råd that I have been studying the Pentateuch, and they asked me many questions about these first five books of the Old Testament. Afterward, I received this note from Chancellor Oxenstierna, who was present during the questioning:

I hope that you will rule over your country for many years, endowed as you are with character and outstanding talents. From your earliest childhood you have been surrounded by the love and respect of your people and the amazed admiration of neighboring countries.

I shall always treasure these words, for the chancellor is not one who gives praise easily or often.

May 4, 1639

Karl has come home, and is much distressed by his mother's failing health. Nevertheless, he leaves next week for his long journey. Aunt Katarina insists upon it. What a sad farewell it will surely be.

May 10, 1639

Early yesterday we said good-bye to Karl. He did not mention anything more about "granting a special place in my affections" — thank goodness! He did say that he will write often, and I promised to reply. He kissed his mother warmly — she has seemed stronger this past week, even joining us for dinner. Then he and his retinue of servants made their way out of the courtyard in carriages headed for Göteborg on the western coast. From there he sails to Rotterdam.

Magnus travels with him. I witnessed De la Gardie's tender parting from Marie Euphrosyne, who seems to be moping over his departure more than is necessary, in my opinion.

May 11, 1639

Aunt Katarina has taken a dramatic turn for the worse. The moment Gunilla brought me word, I hastened to my aunt's bedchamber. She lay still and pale, her face nearly as white as her pillow. Eleonore and Marie Euphrosyne were kneeling by her bedside, holding their younger brother by the hand. Uncle Johann paced at the foot of her bed.

Aunt Katarina turned toward the sound of my voice and opened her eyes, smiled faintly, and closed her eyes again. When her eyes remained closed, I went to Uncle Johann. "What happened?" I asked quietly. "She had seemed better."

He shook his head. "She made the effort for Karl's sake. But I fear she has not much longer."

May 13, 1639

My cousins sometimes join me for lessons with Papa Matthiae, but more often than not, they do not come at all.

And when they do, they are distracted and pay even less attention than usual.

I wish that Karl had not left. Aunt Katarina made a show of being brave and strong until he was safely on his way. Uncle Johann wanders about, his brow deeply furrowed, lost in thought. Gunilla does her best to cheer me, but she has no knack for cheer and, in fact, always seems to look on the gloomy side of things.

May 14, 1639

"What will become of me when she dies?" I whispered to Papa Matthiae on Sunday as we returned from Sabbath services. "Must I go then to live again with my mother?"

"Where you will live is in the hands of the chancellor and the Regents," he replied gravely. "You must trust them to do what is best for you."

It was not what I wanted to hear, but I bit down hard on my lip and said nothing more.

Something else to sadden me: The Riksdag has ended its session and the members have all returned to their country homes. That includes Count Sparre and Ebba. Heaven knows when I shall see her again. She has promised to write, but she dislikes writing letters and will find her promise burdensome.

May 17, 1639

During the night Aunt Katarina called for me. I rushed to her chamber, which reeks of odd smells that I cannot identify. Marie Euphrosyne and Eleonore were with her, but my aunt sent them away with a whispered word.

"Dear Kristina," she murmured, taking my cold hand in her feverish one, and smiled weakly.

I drew a deep breath and gripped her hand tightly.

"Karl," she managed to say. "Karl," she repeated.

I leaned closer. "Is there something you want me to tell him?" I asked, my eyes filling with tears.

"Marry him," she breathed, her last words to me.

Later

My aunt died just an hour ago. I am consumed by sorrow. She has been a mother to me as my own mother never was, and now she is gone.

May 29, 1639

We stumble through our days somehow. The funeral was held without Karl, as was my aunt's wish. Marie Euphrosyne suddenly seems less foolish, and she now behaves like a mother to Adolf Johann. Eleonore attempts to console her father, who seems inconsolable.

I wrote to my mother with news of my aunt's death, but if I expected sympathy (I did not) I was sure to be disappointed. My mother despised Aunt Katarina, and her reply to my letter was, as always, a dose of angry criticism. I try to be patient with her and to concentrate on my studies and not to think too much about the possibility that I may be forced by circumstances to live with her again.

June 3, 1639

Whitsunday fell yesterday, and although we are numb with grief, I sent Margareta off to the wedding of her younger sister, as she has long planned. No doubt I will hear every detail when she returns from her family's farm.

June 5, 1639

For nearly a year I have made it a habit to write in this book during the early morning hours, before the rest of the household is awake and before Papa Matthiae arrives. Sometimes I have recorded additional short entries later in the day when there was much to say and I had time to spare. But for the first time I have dropped all my studies and made this diary my most important task, because something so shocking has occurred that I simply cannot wait until tomorrow morning to write about it. It is this:

<u>My mother has been caught in an act of profound disloyalty to Sweden!</u>

I learned of this only hours ago when Chancellor Oxenstierna arrived in my apartments so consumed with anger that he could scarcely speak. He thrust a letter toward me. "Read this," he commanded. "It was seized from a courier."

The letter, written in German in my mother's hand, is addressed to King Christian IV of Denmark, the country that has been our fiercest rival since even before the time of Gustav Vasa. In the letter my mother begs the Danish king to help her escape from Sweden and to give her refuge.

I read the letter once, quickly, and then a second time,

more slowly, to make sure I understood it. And I read it a third time because I could not believe it.

Oxenstierna's face was so red that I feared he might suffer a fit of apoplexy. This normally calm, disciplined man sputtered when he tried to speak. Finally, he snatched the letter from my hand, threw it down, and stomped on it.

"The dowager queen wishes to commit treason!" he roared. "Plainly, she wishes to marry her dead husband's lifelong enemy!"

I touched his arm and tried to pacify him. "I will do what I can to reason with her," I promised.

He stared at me with bulging eyes. "There is nothing you can do, Kristina."

"It is my duty to try," I said, although I dread this obligation.

June 6, 1639

This is the letter I sent to my mother:

Dearest Lady Mother, my Queen,

I have learned this day of your desire to leave Sweden. I understand the loneliness of your situation at Gripsholm. Therefore I beg you, with all my

heart, to come here to Stockholm, to the Castle of
the Three Crowns, and to give me the pleasure of
your company so that we can discuss this and many
other things as well. Please say that you will do me
that honor and favor.

I signed it, "Your loving and devoted daughter, Kristina
R." and dispatched a messenger by fast horse to Gripsholm
before I could change my mind.

June 8, 1639

In the tumult of the past days, I have nearly forgotten to
write about the wedding of Margareta's sister, Birgit. It
amazes me that so much is made over so little, but I suppose that merely reflects my disdain for the idea of matri-
mony.

The whole event abounds with superstition. According to Margareta, every bride's wish is to be married on
Whitsunday, when she is treated like a queen for the entire
day. She must wear shoes without ties or buckles, in order
to avoid difficult childbirth. After the ceremony she must
go to the barn to milk a cow, to insure that she will always
have milk in her new home. Then the feasting begins: The

wedding guests provide the food — roasted pork, hare, ox, lots of cakes and sweets — and everyone must eat a little of each dish, followed by much drinking of ale and brandy.

After that comes the dancing, until finally the hostess serves a rice porridge, the signal for everyone to go home.

This is all I can remember at present, but I am thoroughly sick of the subject.

June 16, 1639

The messenger returned yesterday with my mother's reply. She will arrive here at Three Crowns Castle within the fortnight. I must have been mad to invite her. She will surely make my life as miserable as she ever has.

Only today did I confess to the chancellor what I have done. He was astonished that I have taken this burden upon myself and asked what I intend to do when the queen arrives.

"Find a way to keep her from fleeing to Denmark," I said, although I have no idea how I will do that.

June 17, 1639

The dream again: *The heart pounds in the golden casket above my mother's bed. I scream and put my hands over my ears. "It is your father's noble heart!" my mother cries. She presses a pillow over my face.*

I cowered in my bed as Gunilla faced each corner of the chamber and made the sign of the Cross. "Be gone, vile creature, in the name of God!" Then she put her arms around me. "That is the first night-mare you have suffered in many months," she said. She blames it on Aunt Katarina's death. I did not tell her the real reason: my mother's letter.

June 21, 1639 — Midsummer Day

Today I received word that my mother is at this very hour making her way toward Stockholm.

Just a year ago, my dear aunt gave me this book and instructed me to "fill it with good and honest words, from your heart as well as your mind." I have tried to do that. And, God give me the strength, I shall continue.

June 24, 1639

A letter from Karl, now in France. He feels quite bereft at the death of his cherished mother, but his letter is also filled with descriptions of all he sees and does. I would give anything to change places with him. I refuse to think of my aunt's last words to me: <u>Marry Karl.</u> Impossible!

June 25, 1639

My mother arrived here last evening, accompanied by her German ladies-in-waiting and a cart laden with trunks filled with their finery. I was at my studies when Margareta ran in with news of the dowager queen's arrival, and I hurried down to greet her.

My mother stared at me as she alighted from her carriage. "Good Lord," she said, looking me up and down. "You look worse than ever, Kristina."

I immediately wished that I had never written a single word to her, but nevertheless I welcomed her warmly to the Castle of the Three Crowns.

Her mood changed instantly, and she unleashed a torrent of tears. It was as though a dam had burst on a river, and it took all the soothing words I could summon to calm her. How am I ever going to bear this woman?

June 26, 1639

My mother has stopped weeping long enough for us to have a brief conversation. If she cannot go back to Germany (her destination, she claims), then will I not permit her to move to the royal castle at Nyköping? I promised to consider her request, thinking it might put her into a better disposition and be a more suitable home for her than Gripsholm. But when I mentioned this idea to the chancellor, who is still so angry that he refuses even to call upon her, he went into another tirade. He pointed out that it is an easy voyage from Nyköping to the island of Gotland, a Danish possession in the Baltic Sea.

"As soon as your back is turned, the dowager queen will be on a Danish ship bound for Copenhagen. The Regents believe that she means to marry King Christian and to have you marry his son."

If Oxenstierna wanted to upset me, he could not have picked a better way than to suggest another marriage candidate. But that is not my main worry at the moment.

I asked what he thought I should tell my mother.

"Send her back to Gripsholm," he said. He promised to appoint a new governor of her household to keep watch over her and to prevent her from going over to the Danes.

June 29, 1639

That advice was easy to give and hard to put into action.

My mother has treated me to some spectacular fits of temper, followed by dramatic demonstrations of deep sorrow. As always, I flee to Papa Matthiae, not just for my lessons, but for relief from my mother's hysterics.

July 10, 1639

I cannot stand it even one more day!

Yesterday, the chancellor promised that, once my mother is settled somewhere, he will take me on a journey through Sweden. He is eager for me to visit our great iron-producing area. It is this promise that keeps me from losing my mind.

July 12, 1639

At last, a brief letter from Ebba. I have written her about all that has happened — my aunt's death, my mother's arrival, my worries — and all she said was, "I am so sorry to hear of your distress." Not a word about her own life. Nothing.

I have never felt so alone and lonely.

July 16, 1639

I do not know what brought about her change of heart, but yesterday, as we returned from Sabbath services, my mother calmly informed me that she plans to leave in three days' time for Gripsholm. She has met the new governor of her household and says she is quite pleased with him.

Can I trust this sudden change?

July 20, 1639

She is gone. We had a quiet parting, with only the smallest trickle of tears, no hysterics, no loud criticism of my dress or manners. Once she is back at Gripsholm, she intends to withdraw with one of her ladies for a period of fasting, prayer, and contemplation, and I must not worry if I hear nothing from her for a while. I can breathe more easily, at least for the present.

July 24, 1639

My name day, the feast of Saint Cristina.

I suppose it is safe to celebrate. The governor sent word that my mother has reached Gripsholm. Now she and Frau von Bülau, who seems to be her closest confidante, have withdrawn into a private chamber for a lengthy fast, vowing to eat nothing but cabbage for an entire week. Why cabbage, I wonder?

July 25, 1639

Gunilla arranged a small dinner in honor of my name day and invited my cousins. Uncle Johann has gone to the Kasimir family castle in Stegeborg, leaving the girls and Adolf Johann here at Three Crowns. They will be in deep mourning for their mother for a year, but they were allowed to dine with me, and I think this small event was good for us all.

My cousins surprised me with an unusual gift: a goldfinch that has been trained to pull a chain with a tiny bucket attached. The bucket is filled with seed or water. When the bird pulls the chain, the bucket empties the contents into a dish, from which he then eats or drinks. Adolf Johann is so entranced with it that I have allowed him to keep the bird in his bedchamber and take care of it for me.

July 27, 1639

Gustav Horn did not appear for my French lessons today. I learned that he died suddenly last night while attending a banquet. I feel terrible about this, for I was fond of him. In the past six months, I have suffered the loss of three people who were important to me, and my heart is sore.

July 31, 1639

I cannot believe what my mother has done! This morning we received a distraught message from the governor: The dowager queen has fled from Gripsholm. He has no idea where she has gone. I think I know: Denmark.

More later.

Sunset

The cabbage may have been real, but the "contemplation" involved the devising of a clever plan of escape. Before sunrise two days ago (the sun rises now at about half past two), my mother and Frau von Bülau lowered themselves from a window into the garden, where a carriage waited for them. There were also two gentlemen, but the governor does not know their identities. Members of her retinue? Danes sent by King Christian? Someone else? The governor promises to find out.

I have sent a message to Uncle Johann at Stegeborg, begging him to come to Three Crowns to discuss this.

August 5, 1639

One piece of the mystery has been solved. We now know that the carriage took my mother and her friend to Nyköping, which she reached by sunset. A Danish skiff waiting there transported them to Gotland, where two Danish warships lay at anchor. According to witnesses, the warships sailed from Gotland the next morning. My mother has not been seen since.

The chancellor is speechless with rage (again!). "This will make us the laughingstock of Europe!" he cries. "The widow of Sweden's greatest king, consorting with the enemy!"

I care not at all if they laugh. I simply want to know where my mother is and what she plans to do next.

August 10, 1639

Uncle Johann has come, and Chancellor Oxenstierna has gone, angry with <u>me</u> now, for sending for my uncle.

It upsets me that the chancellor distrusts the one family connection I still have. Oxenstierna believes that my uncle will try to ingratiate himself further, have Karl appointed to high office, and eventually succeed in convincing me to marry Karl and make him king. I admire the chancellor for all he has done for Sweden and all he has taught me, but I find myself disagreeing with him on many things. I fear we parted on bad terms.

August 15, 1639

Falling, falling. The night-mares gallop through my sleep, and I get little rest because of them. In the mornings, my bones ache as though I really did fall and my head throbs. When Papa Matthiae comes, I shall send him away. I do not know why I feel —

Date??

Mother in Copenhagen. Too weak to write. Gunilla says will write for me. No —

September 10, 1639

Gunilla says today is the tenth, and so that is the date I put down. I have missed my oral examinations. She says I must not worry. Where is Mother? Gunilla says not to think of her now.

September 19, 1639

I am feeling better. My strength is slowly returning. I owe this recovery to a French apothecary, Pierre Bourdelot, sent for by Oxenstierna. Bourdelot believes that my headaches and palpitations and fainting fits, from which I have suffered lately, are due to my diet. He claims that Swedish food is enough to kill anybody and has forbidden me to eat smoked and salted meat. Instead, he has prescribed veal broth to be taken several times a day, barley water, and extracts of lemons and oranges brought from Spain.

September 23, 1639

For weeks, I have scarcely left my bedchamber. Papa Matthiae comes every day but says I am not yet strong enough to continue my studies. The chancellor also visits dutifully, but I feel a growing distance between us.

I have plenty of time to think.

Tomorrow I shall write about my mother.

September 24, 1639

My mother is in Germany. Her nephew, the Elector of Brandenburg, wrote to inform us that she has returned to Berlin. She was not happy in Denmark after all. Now the Elector claims that he is not responsible for her debts and demands that Sweden send money for her support. (This Elector is my cousin, Friedrich Wilhelm, the very same Friedrich Wilhelm whom she wants me to marry.)

All of Sweden is furious at my mother's behavior and is determined to punish her. The Råd refuses to send money to the Elector and will propose to the Riksdag at its next session that her Swedish property be seized.

This makes me feel very sad. She is my mother, after all! But it is a relief not to have her chastising me in front of the entire court, or privately, by letter.

October 1, 1639

At noon today I meet with the Råd for my oral examinations. In a strange way, I am not the same Kristina I was two months ago, before my mother ran away, before I fell ill. I am much stronger, and at last I feel in charge of my own destiny.

October 2, 1639

The Råd assembled in their stark chamber, all those solemn, bearded, black-robed men. They first inquired about the state of my health. They noted that I looked very well and seem to have grown taller and perhaps plumper since the last time they had gathered. I then proceeded to answer their detailed questions about philosophy, religion, history, and anything else, so that they could have no questions about my abilities as a scholar. "As fine as any prince in the world!" they said with obvious satisfaction.

I was expected to smile and accept their gracious compliments. But I did not follow tradition. Instead, I rose and spoke to them from both my head and my heart, as I never have before.

"I know that you are all deeply disappointed, as am I, and gravely troubled, as am I, at the departure of my lady mother, the dowager queen."

I noted the look of surprise when I brought up the subject that every man among them hoped to avoid. "You have decided to seize her property, as you have a right to do," I said in a clear voice. "And you have declined to continue to support the sorrowing widow of your beloved 'Gösta Hooknose,' the Lion of the North, King Gustav Adolf the Great. As you have a right to do."

The black-robed men shifted uneasily in their seats. In the back row sat Oxenstierna, his brow more deeply furrowed than ever. I lifted my chin and spoke more strongly. "You have declined to continue to support the mother of your future monarch. As you have a right to do."

By now, the men were unsure where to look, and so their eyes roved everywhere in the great Hall of State — everywhere but in my direction. "I want you to know that my mother is my responsibility, as she was my father's. I will support her from my own purse. As I have a right to do."

The members froze in total silence. I made a low bow and left the great chamber.

I was not surprised when Oxenstierna showed up in my apartments within the hour. We sat without speaking, until finally the chancellor cleared his throat. "You astonished me today, Kristina," he said. "You astonished us all."

"Probably not for the last time. Now I wish to make some plans."

I told him, first, that I wish to leave soon for the lengthy trip through Sweden, so that I may get to know my country and my subjects. The chancellor nodded his agreement. And then I said that I mean to begin attending meetings of the Råd. He immediately began to protest, but I stopped him.

"You have taught me well," I reminded him. "As a result, I am as fine a scholar as any prince. And I shall be as great a king as any man." I put only a slight emphasis on "king."

He heard me. His bushy eyebrows shot up. There was a long silence as we met each other's gaze. Then Chancellor Oxenstierna dropped to his creaky old knees. "I am obedient to your wishes, my king," he said.

I smiled. This was the first time he addressed me as <u>king</u>. It will not be the last.

Epilogue

The next few years were lonely ones for Kristina. With her hysterical mother in Germany and her beloved aunt dead, she was surrounded by elderly men who had no idea how to bring up this brilliant but strong-willed girl. She threw herself more intensely than ever into her studies. She so impressed the Råd that they urged her to begin her rule even before she came of age. But, recognizing the burden that would be placed upon her, Kristina declined. Nevertheless, on her eighteenth birthday, December 8, 1644, Kristina took the oath as king and prepared to rule.

In 1648, Kristina's mother returned from Germany, took up residence at Nyköping Castle, and resumed her nagging — especially on the subject of marriage.

Speculation about a future husband for Kristina increased. Her cousin, Karl, wanted to marry her, but she made it plain that she would not marry Karl or anyone else. She did, however, name him her successor to the throne.

By 1650, Kristina was seriously involved in her intellectual pursuits. She corresponded with the French thinker René Descartes and invited him to Stockholm. She was also already secretly coming to a momentous decision: to give up the throne. She found the burden of governing exhausting and the restrictions on her personal freedom maddening. But there was another, deeper reason: She had decided to convert to Catholicism. Because Sweden was a Lutheran country, she could not become a Catholic and remain on the Swedish throne. Amid protests from the Riksdag, Kristina announced her decision to abdicate.

On the sixth of June 1654, she appeared in the Hall of State at Uppsala Castle where she had been officially enthroned less than four years earlier on October 20, 1650. Wearing the crown and carrying the orb and scepter, she addressed the members of the Riksdag. When Chancellor Oxenstierna could not bring himself to remove the crown from her head, she removed it herself, curtsied to Prince Karl, who would shortly be crowned king, and left the vast hall. This deeply emotional occasion marked the end of that part of Kristina's life.

She left Sweden and traveled through Europe, attracting attention with her flamboyant manner. She rode astride. She refused to be accompanied by a chaperone. She dressed in men's clothes. Eventually, she moved on to Rome, where she was baptized in the Catholic Church on Christmas Eve of 1654. She took as her name "Christina Alexandra."

The loyal Axel Oxenstierna died a brokenhearted man a few months after Kristina's abdication. The following year, 1655, Kristina's mother died. Johannes Matthiae, who had been named Bishop of Strångnås when his royal pupil came of age, was blamed for her conversion to Catholicism and was stripped of his title. Soon after his coronation, King Karl X married a German princess recommended by Kristina. Magnus De la Gardie married Marie Euphrosyne, and Magnus's younger brother, Jakob, married Kristina's dear friend, Ebba Sparre.

Kristina died on April 19, 1689, at the age of sixty-two. She had requested a simple funeral and burial, but her close friend, Cardinal Decio Azzolino, went against her wishes and arranged for her to be buried in St. Peter's, the first foreign monarch to be interred there beside the popes of the church.

Historians argue that, although she is the most discussed of all queens in history, second only to Cleopatra, Kristina actually achieved very little during her brief reign. But present-day admirers describe Kristina as a feminist and a rebel, a woman with radical ideas who rejected the feminine ideals of her time. In an age when men and women were willing to risk their lives for the right to wear the crown, Kristina chose to give up a kingdom for the freedom to live as she wished.

Life in Sweden

Historical Note

Queen Maria Eleonora was right: At the time of Kristina's birth, Sweden was a remote and backward place only thinly populated by superstitious peasants and a small number of poorly educated noblemen. But Kristina's father, King Gustav II Adolf, believed that under his leadership this far northern kingdom with its dark and frigid winters was destined to become the center of a Baltic empire that would dominate Europe. His means to accomplish this goal was through military conquest.

War as the way of expanding one's territory was not a new idea, even among the tall, blond, blue-eyed Svear who inhabited what is now known as Sweden (*Sverige* in Swedish). In the seventh century A.D., fierce warrior-seamen called Vikings swept in from the north, overran the Svear, and established a settlement, called Birka, on the shore of Lake Mälaren. In fast, brightly painted longboats propelled by two dozen or more oarsmen and a single, striped square sail, the Vikings crisscrossed the Baltic Sea. They carried their boats over long portages to rivers leading into the heartland of Eastern Europe and Russia, reaching Byzantium and Baghdad, and trading on what is now called the Silk Road, the trade route that led all the way to China.

The Vikings lived in a collection of small, autonomous kingdoms, each ruled by a minor king, and worshiped a pantheon of pagan gods. Not until the eleventh century did Christianity begin to make serious inroads; even so, pagan superstitions persisted for hundreds of years. The Christian idea of one God rather than many evolved into the idea of one king ruling over all. As a result, there were now many bloody battles for supremacy. In the twelfth century, King Erik IX led a crusade through Finland; he is considered the patron saint of Sweden.

An outbreak of the plague in the fourteenth century brought death to a third of the inhabitants of Sweden, and the country was badly weakened. That century was also marked with increased conflict between Sweden and its neighbors, until in 1397 Queen Margarethe of Denmark brought together Denmark, Sweden, and Norway in the Kalmar Union for a few decades of stability. But after her death, loyalties began to shift and promises were forgotten. Over a period of a half century, Denmark attacked Sweden repeatedly. In the infamous "Stockholm Bloodbath" of 1520, the Danes declared an amnesty and then treacherously beheaded a number of Swedish noblemen. It was in this atmosphere that Gustav Eriksson rose to become King Gustav I Vasa three years later.

Gustav I Vasa modernized the Swedish army and seized church property to pay the bills. He married three times and produced three sons who succeeded him — Erik, Johan, and Karl. There were bad relations between Gustav's three sons, especially between Erik and his oldest half brother, Johan. (Erik XIV once imprisoned his brother, Prince Johan, and his bride, the sister of the king of Poland. Four years later, in 1568, he freed them. Erik is said to have died of poison in his pea soup, put there by Johan, who was then crowned Johan III.) Karl, the youngest and last surviving, was crowned officially in 1604. Karl IX died before reaching his goal of ruling all of the Baltic region; his son, Gustav Adolf, was determined to continue his father's objectives.

Gustav II Adolf proved to be a military genius as well as an ambitious king. First, he ended a war with Denmark and Norway and recaptured parts of southern Sweden. Next, he attacked Poland and seized control of the Polish Baltic coast. Then, in 1618, King Gustav II Adolf plunged his country into a struggle in Germany that would last for the next thirty years.

The war began as a religious conflict between Protestants and Roman Catholics. It quickly turned political, with the powerful Catholic Hapsburg family attempting to wrest control of much of Europe away from the now Protestant princes.

King Gustav II Adolf, a devout Lutheran, continued to fight his war against Catholic Poland but was killed in a battle in Germany in 1632. His crown passed to his daughter, Kristina, his only child. Regents governing for Kristina continued her father's military policies. However, in 1648, Kristina signed the Treaty of Westphalia, officially ending what is known today as the Thirty Years War. The long war had left the country impoverished and the population devastated by the loss of life, although many noblemen serving as field commanders returned home in glory, rich enough to build great mansions near the royal palace. Among the peasants, Sweden had thousands of "jackwidows," women whose husbands had been killed on the battlefield. It would be years before Sweden recovered socially and economically.

During her relatively short reign, Kristina tried to raise Sweden to the intellectual level of other European countries, inviting to her court a steady stream of philosophers, scientists, and mathematicians. A journey to Sweden was considered a perilous adventure by Europeans;

the winter trip from Copenhagen to Stockholm could take as long as six weeks through ice and snow. Perhaps the most famous guest to accept the royal invitation was the French philosopher, René Descartes. Ordered to meet with Kristina in her library in the very early hours of the morning during the numbingly cold Swedish winter, the frail and elderly philosopher succumbed to pneumonia before spring arrived.

Kristina was admired widely as a highly learned woman, often called "Minerva of the North," for the Roman goddess of wisdom and the arts. Her abdication and subsequent conversion to Catholicism shocked not only Sweden but all of Europe. She settled in Rome, where she was honored as a patron of the arts, but again found herself the center of controversy when she became embroiled in Vatican politics.

Kristina visited Sweden briefly in 1660 to attend the funeral of her cousin and successor, King Karl X. Seven years later, she visited a second time. When it was discovered that she traveled with a Catholic priest in her retinue, the Regents for the thirteen-year-old King Karl XI halted Kristina on her way to Stockholm and decreed that she could not enter Sweden until the boy reached the age of eighteen.

Kristina never returned to her homeland again.

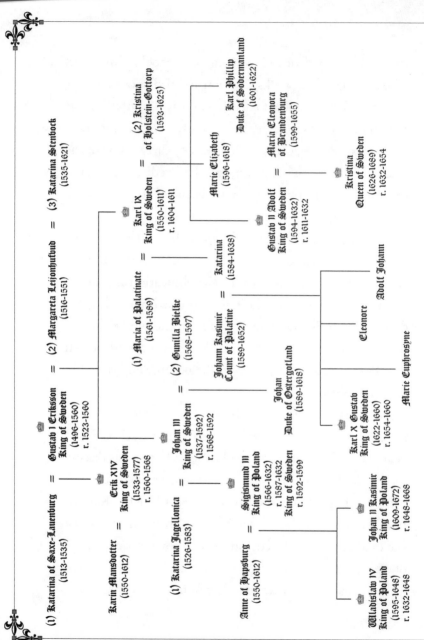

The Vasa-Palatinate Family Tree

The Vasa royal kingship began with Gustav Eriksson who was elected King Gustav I Vasa of Sweden (r. 1523–60) after he led a heroic revolt against the rule of Denmark. Gustav I made the kingship hereditary, passing the crown to his first son, then his second and third.

Kristina, an only child, worked diligently to make herself a Vasa king. She succeeded her father, Gustav II Adolf (r. 1611–32), at age six, and assumed the kingship in 1644 upon her eighteenth birthday. When Kristina I abdicated the crown in 1654, she selected her Palatinate cousin, Karl X Gustav (r. 1654–60) as her successor.

The chart portrays the development of the Vasa-Palatinate royal descent from the sixteenth to the seventeenth centuries. The crown symbol indicates those who ruled. Double lines represent marriages; single lines indicate parentage. Dates of births and deaths (when available) are noted.

𝕲𝖚𝖘𝖙𝖆𝖇 𝟏 𝕰𝖗𝖎𝖐𝖘𝖘𝖔𝖓 𝖁𝖆𝖘𝖆: Elected King of Sweden in 1523, he reformed the economy and administration of the state, made Lutheranism the state religion, and, in 1544, made his heirs hereditary kings.

Children of 𝕲𝖚𝖘𝖙𝖆𝖇 𝟏 𝕰𝖗𝖎𝖐𝖘𝖘𝖔𝖓

𝕰𝖗𝖎𝖐 𝐗𝐈𝐕: The son of Gustav I and his first wife, Katarina of Saxe-Lauenburg, he became king upon his father's death. He was overthrown by his brothers and died from poison in prison.

𝕵𝖔𝖍𝖆𝖓 𝐈𝐈𝐈: The first — and favorite — son of Gustav I and his second wife, Margareta Leijonhufvud. Johan married the Catholic sister of King Sigismund II of Poland without his brother King Erik XIV's blessing. Erik imprisoned Johan and his wife, Katarina Jagellonica. Released in 1568, Johan joined with some unhappy nobles and his brother Karl to overthrow Erik and make himself king. His son Sigismund was made the Catholic King of Poland in 1587.

𝕶𝖆𝖗𝖑 𝐈𝐗: Kristina's grandfather and the youngest son of Gustav I and his second wife. Karl, who was the able duke of Södermanland, Närke, and Västmanland led the Swedish peasants against his nephew Sigismund to win the crown by 1600. He was known as "King of the Peasants." Karl IX and his first wife, Maria of Palatinate, had a daughter, Katarina. His second wife was Kristina of Holstein-Gottorp. Together they had three children: Gustav Adolf (Kristina's father), Marie Elizabeth, and Karl Phillip.

Family of Kristina I Vasa

Gustav II Adolf: Kristina's father, was the first son of Karl IX. When Karl IX died, Gustav II was sixteen and already an experienced coruler. Gustav II spoke seven languages and quickly showed himself to be a great military strategist, winning the three wars he inherited. Known as Gustav the Great, he adored his only child, Kristina.

Maria Eleonora of Brandenburg: Kristina's mother, was the daughter of Johann Sigismund, Elector of Brandenburg (1572–1619), and Anna, heiress of Preussen (Prussia, 1576–1625). It is said that there was a history of madness, melancholy, and overindulgence in her family. She lost three children at birth or during infancy before the birth of Kristina.

Kristina I Vasa: Born December 8, 1626, in Stockholm. In 1632, upon her father's death, Kristina inherited the Swedish crown. During her reign, she assembled a Court of Learning to which she invited the greatest scholars and artists of the day, including René Descartes. The first newspaper in Sweden was established, and Kristina played a central role, in 1648, in ending the Thirty Years War. Kristina abdicated her throne in favor of her Palatinate cousin, Karl Gustav, in 1654 and by the next year had converted to Catholicism. She moved to Rome, where she died on April 19, 1689.

Other Royals in the Vasa-Palatinate Family

Katarina Vasa, Countess Palatine: Kristina's aunt, the half-sister of King Gustav II Adolf. Katarina was the only child to live to adulthood from Karl IX's first marriage to Maria of Palatinate.

Johann Kasimir, Count Palatine: Kristina's uncle. Born in Zwëibrucken, Pfalz, Bavaria, the Count Palatine lived in Sweden from the time of his marriage, in 1615, to Katarina, Princess of Sweden.

Karl, Duke of Zwëibrucken-Kleeburg: Kristina's cousin. Eldest son of Katarina Vasa and Johann Kasimir. He was named King Karl X Gustav of Sweden when his cousin abdicated the Swedish throne. In 1654, he married Marie Eleanore of Holstein-Gottorp. Their only son, Karl XI, became King of Sweden in 1660 at age five when his father died suddenly.

Portrait of fifteen-year-old Kristina by court painter Jakob Henrik Elbfas, circa 1641. From an early age, Kristina loathed the time-consuming process of having her portrait painted.

*Kristina's mother,
Queen Maria Eleonora.
Although she loved her daughter,
Maria Eleonora was
emotionally unstable and was
eventually stripped of any
parental rights over Kristina.*

*A 1627 painting
of King Gustav II Adolf,
Kristina's father.*

Countess Katarina, Gustav Adolf's half sister and Kristina's beloved aunt, functioned as a second mother to the young monarch.

Portrait of Kristina's tutor, Johannes Matthiae. She regarded him as a father figure, calling him "Papa Matthiae."

Chancellor Axel Oxenstierna. Charged with supervising Kristina until she turned eighteen, he made most of the decisions concerning her education and even determined the frequency of interactions between the young ruler and her mother.

This dramatic illustration depicts six-year-old Kristina's accession of the Swedish throne. Although most of the Swedish Regents exhibited their support, some court members were outraged at the notion of a female child being the sole ruler of the country.

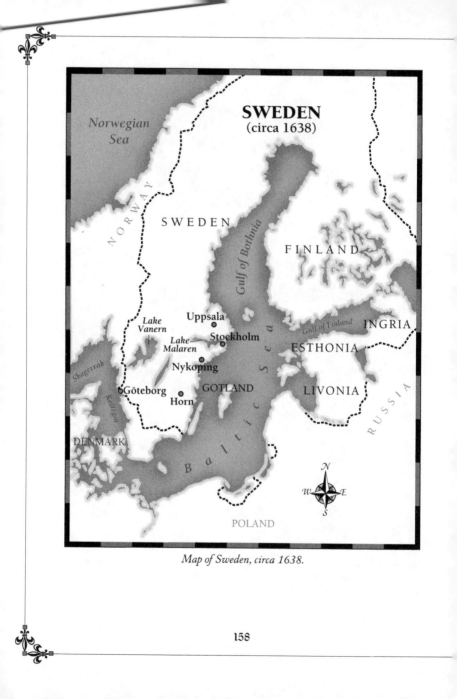

Map of Sweden, circa 1638.

Rendering of Three Crowns Castle, located in Stockholm. This enormous edifice was initially constructed as a fortress. Gustav Vasa was the first king to use the fortress as a residence, and during the reign of King Johan III, it was transformed into a wondrous palace. Tragically, in 1697, most of the castle was destroyed in a devastating fire. Plans were made to redesign and rebuild the structure, but it took sixty years to actually finish construction.

A modern-day Swedish postage stamp (top) *and a silver coin* (bottom) *each present different likenesses of Kristina. Seemingly a common occurrence, numerous artists created extraordinarily diverse images of her physical appearance.*

Kristina, in 1687, at the age of sixty, painted by artist Michael Dahl. After abdicating the throne in 1654, she turned her attentions to areas of philosophy and religion. Her social circle included some of the greatest thinkers and philosophers of the time, including René Descartes.

The tomb of Kristina in the Church of St. Peter in Rome. She died in Rome, in 1689, at the age of sixty-two.

Glossary of Characters

(*denotes fictional character)

VASA FAMILY:

King Gustav Eriksson Vasa — Kristina's great-grandfather

Erik IV, Johan III, Karl IX — sons of King Gustav Vasa

King Gustav II Adolf — son of King Karl IX; Kristina's father

Maria Eleonora of Brandenburg — wife of Gustav II Adolf; Kristina's mother

KASIMIR FAMILY:

Katarina Kasimir — sister of Gustav II Adolf; Kristina's aunt

Johann Kasimir — husband of Katarina; Kristina's uncle

Karl, Marie Euphrosyne, Eleonore, Adolf Johann — Kasimir children; Kristina's cousins

Oxenstierna family:

Axel Oxenstierna — chancellor; Gustav II Adolf's closest friend; Kristina's advisor

Beate — Axel's wife

Oxenstierna nieces (unnamed) — Kristina's ladies-in-waiting

De la Gardie family:

Jakob De la Gardie (elder) — member of Swedish nobility

Ebba (Brahe) De la Gardie — Jakob's wife; once Gustav II Adolf's sweetheart

Magnus De la Gardie — eldest son of Jakob and Ebba; friend of Karl Kasimir and Kristina

Jakob De la Gardie (younger) — younger brother of Magnus

Tutors and governors:

Johannes Matthiae — chaplain to Gustav II Adolf; Kristina's tutor

Axel Banér — Kristina's governor in military arts

Gustav Horn — Kristina's governor in languages

Signor Tagliaferro (*) — instructor in fencing

Jakob Henrik Elbfas — court painter

Antoine de Beaulieu — instructor in ballet

NURSES, SERVANTS, AND OTHERS:

Margareta (*) — serving maid

Gunilla (*) — Kristina's new nurse

Frau Anna — Kristina's first infant nurse

Pierre Bourdelot — French apothecary

Lars Larsson — peasant in Riksdag

Lars Sparre — noble member of Riksdag

Ebba Sparre — daughter of Lars Sparre; Kristina's closest
    friend

About the Author

"I love books and I love movies, and I'm fascinated by how different the two can be, even when they're dealing with the same subject," says author Carolyn Meyer.

When Ms. Meyer began to research the life of Kristina of Sweden, she watched an old Greta Garbo movie, filmed in 1933, titled *Queen Christina*. "The story wasn't just a little different, it was *completely* different. In the film she gave up the throne — not to convert to Catholicism, but in order to marry a Spanish nobleman, who then fought in a duel and died in her arms. This never happened in the life of the real Kristina. There were also small inaccuracies, like the bountiful bowls of fruit shown in one scene of the movie — fruit that couldn't grow in Sweden's cold climate. In essence, the filmmakers made a film which, while entertaining, has almost nothing to do with the real Kristina."

Ms. Meyer believes that accuracy in historical fiction is very important, but she admits that sometimes changes do have to be made for the sake of the story. The diary stays true to events in Kristina's life, though some *sequences* of events are shifted. For example, Sweden's first ballet was really performed in January of 1638. In another instance, Kristina's mother, Dowager Queen Maria Eleonora, actually fled from Sweden to Denmark in 1640. Often, too, the facts are not clear: Most sources mention only four Kasimir cousins — Karl, Marie Euphrosyne, Eleonore, and Johann; several Internet sites have turned up a fifth cousin but provide no details of her life besides the dates of her birth (ten years before Kristina was born) and her death at a late age.

"It is always a challenge to pick and choose among the various possibilities, in order to give the clearest, most interesting, and most accurate portrayal of a historical figure," Ms. Meyer remarks. "I embraced the challenge to present this brilliant young girl who inherited the crown and then gave it all up to live the life she wanted."

Kristina: The Girl King is Carolyn Meyer's third book for The Royal Diaries series. *Anastasia, The Last Grand Duchess,* followed her debut title *Isabel, Jewel of Castilla.* The best-selling author of historical fiction has written about fifty books for middle-grade and young adult readers. She resides with her husband in Albuquerque, New Mexico.

Acknowledgments

Grateful acknowledgment is made for permission to reprint the following:

Cover painting by Tim O'Brien.

Page 153: Kristina, Statens Konstmuseer, Swedish Portrait Archives, National Museum, Stockholm, Sweden.

Page 154 (top): Queen Maria Eleonora, Statens Konstmuseer, Swedish Portrait Archives, National Museum, Stockholm, Sweden.

Page 154 (bottom): King Gustav II Adolf, Statens Konstmuseer, Swedish Portrait Archives, National Museum, Stockholm, Sweden.

Page 155: Countess Katarina, Statens Konstmuseer, Swedish Portrait Archives, National Museum, Stockholm, Sweden.

Page 156 (top): Johannes Matthiae, Statens Konstmuseer, Swedish Portrait Archives, National Museum, Stockholm, Sweden.

Page 156 (bottom): Axel Oxenstierna, Statens Konstmuseer, Swedish Portrait Archives, National Museum, Stockholm, Sweden.

Page 157: Illustration of accession of throne, Culver Pictures, New York, New York.

Page 158: Map of Sweden, Jim McMahon.

Other books in The Royal Diaries Series

Elizabeth I
Red Rose of the House of Tudor
by Kathryn Lasky

Cleopatra VII
Daughter of the Nile
by Kristiana Gregory

Marie Antoinette
Princess of Versailles
by Kathryn Lasky

Isabel
Jewel of Castilla
by Carolyn Meyer

Anastasia
The Last Grand Duchess
by Carolyn Meyer

Nzingha
Warrior Queen of Matamba
by Patricia C. McKissack

Kaiulani
The People's Princess
by Ellen Emerson White

LADY OF CH'IAO KUO
Warrior of the South
by Laurence Yep

VICTORIA
May Blossom of Britannia
by Anna Kirwan

MARY, QUEEN OF SCOTS
Queen without a Country
by Kathryn Lasky

SONDOK
Princess of the Moon and Stars
by Sheri Holman

JAHANARA
Princess of Princesses
by Kathryn Lasky

ELEANOR
Crown Jewel of Aquitaine
by Kristiana Gregory

ELISABETH
The Princess Bride
by Barry Denenberg

For Lianna, Danielle, and Shannon

Copyright © 2003 by Carolyn Meyer.

All rights reserved. Published by Scholastic Inc.
557 Broadway, New York, NY 10012.
SCHOLASTIC, THE ROYAL DIARIES and associated logos are trademarks and/or registered trademarks of Scholastic Inc.

Library of Congress Cataloging-in-Publication Data available.

ISBN 0-439-24976-7

10 9 8 7 6 5 4 3 2 1   03 04 05 06 07

The display type was done in Cloister Black.
The text type was set in Augereau.
Book design by Elizabeth B. Parisi
Photo research by Amla Sanghvi
and Sara-Maria Vischer Masino.

Printed in the U.S.A.   23
First printing, May 2003